Netochka Nezvanova

Netochka Nezvanova

BY

FYODOR DOSTOYEVSKY

Translated by Ann Dunnigan

PRENTICE-HALL, INC.
Englewood Cliffs, N.J.

NETOCHKA NEZVANOVA
by Fyodor Dostoyevsky
© 1970 by Ann Dunnigan for this translation
Copyright under International and Pan-American
Copyright Conventions

First PRISM PAPERBACK edition, 1971

ISBN: 0-13-611731-7

Library of Congress Catalog Card Number: 76-113048

Printed in the United States of America
10 9 8 7 6 5 4 3 2 1

Prentice-Hall International, Inc., London
Prentice-Hall of Australia, Pty. Ltd., Sydney
Prentice-Hall of Canada, Ltd., Toronto
Prentice-Hall of India Private Limited, New Delhi
Prentice-Hall of Japan, Inc.

Netochka Nezvanova was to have been Dostoyevsky's first full-length novel—the first-person story of a woman's life. The reason it was terminated at its present length is as dramatic as any incident in the book itself.

Fyodor Mikhailovich Dostoyevsky was born on October 30, 1821, in Moscow. Twenty-three years later, he set out in earnest to begin a writer's career. His early pieces—*Poor Folk, The Double, The Landlady*—established his reputation as a creator of short fiction which made up in power and emotional intensity for what it may have lacked in symmetry and economy. Then, in 1846, he began work on *Netochka Nezvanova.*

He was able to complete approximately half of his first projected masterpiece, bringing Netochka to the verge of womanhood. But in April of 1849, Dostoyevsky was imprisoned in the Fortress of Saint Peter and Saint Paul: the police did not look kindly on his admiration for the radical Petrachevsky, who had captured the writer's attention back in 1847.

Three days before Christmas of 1849, Dostoyevsky was condemned to death. He was within sight of the scaffold when he learned that his sentence had been commuted—to Siberian exile. He began the long, bitter journey on Christmas Eve; the first installment of *Netochka Nezvanova* had appeared only a few months before.

Ten years later, Tsar Alexander II ascended to the throne, and Dostoyevsky returned from exile with the wife he had married in 1858. He was free to take up *Netochka Nezvanova* where he had left off. But now, after intimate association with criminals, thieves, murderers, political prisoners—the most wretched of Russian society—Dostoyevsky's thoughts were turning elsewhere, to the grand and complex questions of guilt and expiation that were to infuse his *Crime and Punishment* and *The Brothers*

Karamazov. Not that he had outgrown *Netochka Nezvanova,* but its theme of victimized innocence was one which the author had explored sufficiently in his own life. From now on, his "saintly" characters—Alyosha in *Brothers Karamazov,* the Princely *Idiot*—would not be as helpless as little Netochka, but active participants on the side of grace. *Netochka Nezvanova* remains, then, as a pivotal work of Dostoyevsky's career, the last creation of his more romantic, undisciplined imagination.

But if Netochka is too young to resist the often appalling conditions that beset her, her life is hardly the less enthralling. Indeed, this first-person narrative leads the reader through a number of Dostoyevsky's most strongly-felt conflicts: the artistic vanity of Netochka's drunken father; her "adoption" by a generous nobleman; her humiliation and torment at the hands of the beautiful little Princess Katya; her final, shocking discovery of the secret beneath the vicious, agonized marriage of Katya's married sister. Netochka's emotions are continually abraded between cruelty and tenderness, pride and humility, devotion and infidelity, patience and rage; poverty, abandonment, and nascent sexuality. In the words of Ann Dunnigan, *Netochka Nezvanova* "shows how the formation and deformation of character are determined in childhood by deliberate and unthinking acts. . . .Literary historians and critics never fail to mention this work as remarkable for its psychological penetration, for its acute analysis of a child's awakening emotions, and its seminal relation to the later novels."

In this new translation, a few minor stylistic changes have been effected to make Dostoyevsky's narrative more accessible to the modern reader. Space breaks have been introduced to reinforce the passage of time, for example; and Dostoyevsky's paragraphs—often extremely long in the original Russian text—have been broken down into smaller units, in confirmation with twentieth century conventions. *Netochka Nezvanova* is best presented, we believe, with a memory to its original, serial appearance in 1849—as an intensely dramatic story whose insights and rich texture were not intended to be savored at a single sitting.

Englewood Cliffs, N. J.

Netochka Nezvanova

ONE

$\mathcal{I}$ do not remember my father; he died when I was two years old. My mother married again, and though she married for love this second marriage brought her great suffering. My stepfather was a musician. He was the strangest, most extraordinary man I have ever known, and had a most unusual fate. His influence on the earliest impressions of my childhood was far too power-ful—so powerful in fact that these impressions have affected my entire life. To make my story understandable, I shall first give an account of his life. All that I now relate I learned only later from the famous violinist B, the companion and close friend of his youth.

My stepfather's surname was Yefimov. He was born in the village of a rich landowner, to a poor musician who, after a life of wandering, had settled on the landowner's estate and was hired to play in his orchestra. The landowner lived very luxuriously and had a passionate, a surpassing love for music. The story was told of him that, though he never left his country estate even to go to Moscow, one day he suddenly decided to spend a few weeks abroad at a spa for the sole purpose of hearing a certain famous violinist who, as he had learned from the newspapers, intended to give three concerts there. He had a rather good orchestra of his own, on which he spent almost his entire income, and it was for this orchestra that my stepfather was engaged as a clarinetist.

When he was twenty-two years old, my stepfather made the acquaintance of a very strange man. In the same district lived a rich count who had ruined himself maintaining a private theater. This Count had dismissed his orchestra leader, an Italian by birth, for misconduct. The orchestra leader was, in fact, an evil man. After his dismissal he became completely debased and began frequenting village taverns, getting drunk, and begging for money, till eventually no one in the entire province would give him work. And it was with this man that my stepfather became friendly. There was something odd and inexplicable about the relationship, in that no one seemed to notice that my stepfather had in any way changed as a consequence of imitating his companion. Even the landowner, who at first had forbidden him to associate with the Italian, subsequently closed his eyes to their friendship.

Then one day the orchestra leader suddenly died. He was found by some peasants one morning in a ditch near the milldam. An inquest was held, and it was found that he had died of apoplexy. His belongings had been left for safekeeping with my stepfather, who immediately presented proof that he was fully entitled to inherit them: the deceased had left a note written in his own hand in which he named Yefimov his heir in the event of his death. The inheritance consisted of a black dress suit, carefully preserved by the Italian, who had not given up hope of obtaining a place in an orchestra, and a quite ordinary-looking violin. No one contested the will.

Only after some time had passed did the first violinist of the Count's orchestra appear with a letter from his master to the landowner. In this letter the Count urgently requested that Yefimov sell him the violin that had been left to him by the Italian, as he was most eager to acquire it for his own orchestra. He offered three thousand rubles, and further stated that he had several times sent for Yegor Yefimov so that he might personally conclude the bargain with him, but that he had stubbornly refused to come. The Count ended by saying that this was the actual cost of the violin, that he had not reduced it, and that he detected in Yefimov's obstinacy the suspicion, insulting to himself, that his simplicity and ignorance were being taken advantage of by this offer. He therefore asked that he be brought to reason.

The landowner immediately sent for my stepfather.

"Why are you unwilling to give up the violin?" he asked him. "It's of no use to you. You will be given three thousand rubles, which is what the violin cost, and if you think you'll get more, you're being unreasonable. The Count wouldn't cheat you."

Yefimov replied that he would not go to the Count of his own accord, but that if he were sent to him, such would be the master's will; that he would not sell the violin to the Count, but if they wanted to take it away from him by force, that too would be the master's will.

It was clear that by such a reply he had touched upon the most sensitive chord of the landowner's nature. As a matter of fact, the landowner had always prided himself on knowing how to treat his musicians, for, as he said, every last one of them was an artist, and it was thanks to them that his orchestra was not only better than the Count's but as good as that of the capital.

"Very well," he said. "I shall inform the Count that you won't sell the violin because you don't wish to, and that you have a perfect right to sell it or not as you please—is that clear? But I myself should like to ask: what good is it to you? The clarinet is your instrument—though you're a wretched clarinetist. Let me have the violin. I'll give you three thousand for it. . . . And anyway, who knows what sort of instrument it may be!"

Yefimov smiled. "No, sir, I won't sell it to you," he replied. "Of course, it's in your power to——"

"Do you think I'm going to compel you—to force you?" shouted the landowner, beside himself with anger, and especially because of the presence of one of the Count's musicians, who having witnessed such a scene might draw exceedingly adverse conclusions about the lot of all the members of the landowner's orchestra.

"Get out of here, you ungrateful creature! Don't let me set eyes on you again! But for me, what would have become of you and that clarinet of yours—which you don't even know how to play? You are well-fed and well-clothed here, and you receive a salary; you live respectably, you're an artist, but you refuse to understand all this, you're not even aware of it! Get out of here and don't exasperate me any longer with your presence!"

Whenever anyone excited his anger the landowner turned the man out, afraid of his own violent temper. Not for anything in the world would he want to be too severe with "an artist," as he called every one of his musicians.

The bargain was not concluded, and that seemed to be the end of the matter, when suddenly, a month later, the Count's violinist instigated a dreadful affair. On his own responsibility, he lodged a complaint against my stepfather in which he attested that he had been guilty of the death of the Italian, whom he had killed out of interested motives: to obtain a rich inheritance. He contended that the will had been made under duress and promised to produce witnesses to the claim. Neither the pleas and exhortations of the landowner and Count, both of whom interceded on behalf of my stepfather, nor anything else could deter the accuser from his purpose. It was explained to him that the proper medical examination had been performed on the body of the deceased orchestra leader, and that in impeaching the evidence he was perhaps motivated by personal vindictiveness and resentment at not having acquired the valuable instrument they had tried to buy for him. The musician stood his ground, swore he was right, held that the stroke had been caused not by drunkeness but by poisoning, and demanded that another inquest be performed.

On the face of it his allegations looked serious, and, inevitably, legal action was taken. Yefimov was arrested and sent to the municipal jail. And there began a case that excited the interest of the whole province. It proceeded very rapidly and ended in the musician's being convicted of making a false denunciation. He was sentenced to a fitting punishment, but stood his ground to the end, claiming that he had been in the right. Subsequently he admitted that he had had no proof whatever, that he had invented the evidence he presented, that in concocting it he had acted on supposition, on conjecture, as up to the time of the second inquest when Yefimov's innocence had been formally proved, he had been fully convinced that Yefimov was responsible for the death of the unfortunate orchestra leader—though he had perhaps not killed him by poison, but by some other means. But before they had time to carry out the sentence on him, he unexpectedly fell ill with inflammation of the brain, went out of his mind, and died in the prison hospital.

The landowner behaved nobly throughout the whole affair, endeavoring to help my stepfather as if he were his own son. He went to see him several times while he was in jail, tried to comfort him, gave him money, took him the finest cigars when he found out that he liked to smoke, and gave the entire orchestra a holiday when he was acquitted. He regarded the matter as something that concerned them all, as he prized the conduct of his musicians as much as if not more than their talent.

A whole year had passed when suddenly a rumor spread through the province that a certain famous violinist, a Frenchman, had arrived in the city and planned to give several concerts while he was there. The landowner immediately tried to find some way of getting him to come to his estate. His efforts succeeded, and the Frenchman promised to come. But after everything had been prepared for his visit and virtually the entire district invited, matters suddenly took a different turn.

It was reported one morning that Yefimov had disappeared and no one knew where he had gone. A search was begun, but no trace of him could be found. The orchestra was in the odd predicament of being without a clarinetist. Then suddenly, three days after Yefimov's disappearance, the landowner received a letter from the Frenchman. In this letter, after arrogantly declining the invitation he had previously accepted, he added—by implication, of course—that in future he would be extremely wary in his relations with gentlemen who maintained their own orchestras; that it offended his aesthetic sensibilities to see a genuine talent under the direction of a man incapable of appreciating its worth; and, finally, that the example of Yefimov, a real artist and the best violinist he had ever encountered in Russia, served as ample proof of the justness of his remarks.

Having read the letter, the landowner was absolutely dumfounded. He felt profoundly mortified. That Yefimov, the man for whom he had gone to so much trouble and to whom he had been such a benefactor—that this same man could ruthlessly and unscrupulously slander him, and to a European artist, a man whose opinion he valued so highly! And for that matter, the letter was baffling in another respect: it stated that Yefimov was an artist of genuine talent, a *violinist,* but that they were incapable of discerning his talent and had forced him to play another instrument. All this so staggered the landowner that he hastily prepared to go to the city to talk to the Frenchman. But suddenly a note came from the Count asking him to come and see him at once. He informed him that the whole affair was known to him, that both the visiting virtuoso and Yefimov were there at his house, as, in his astonishment at the latter's effrontery and slanderous remarks, he had had him detained. In closing, he explained that the landowner's presence was required because Yefimov's imputations involved the Count himself, which was an exceedingly serious matter and would have to be cleared up as soon as possible.

The landowner immediately set off for the Count's estate, where he made the Frenchman's acquaintance and lost no time in telling him my stepfather's whole history, adding that he had never suspected him of having any great talent, that, on the contrary, when Yefimov had been with him he was a very poor clarinetist, and this was the first he had heard of his being a violinist. He also said that Yefimov was a free man, had always enjoyed unqualified liberty, and could have left him at any time had he really felt oppressed.

The Frenchman was astounded. They sent for Yefimov, who when he appeared was hardly recognizable. He was insolent, replied mockingly to their questions, and insisted on the veracity of every slanderous remark he had made to the Frenchman. All this exasperated the Count to the utmost, and he told my stepfather straight out that he was a scoundrel and a traducer and deserved the most humiliating punishment.

"Don't worry, Your Excellency, I'm pretty well acquainted with you by now—I know you very well," retorted my stepfather. "Thanks to you, I barely escaped a criminal sentence. I know at whose instigation Aleksei Nikiforovich, your former musician, denounced me!"

The Count was beside himself with rage at hearing such a frightful accusation. He could hardly control himself, but a government official who had come to see him on business happened to be in the room and declared that he could not let this pass without taking action, that Yefimov's insulting rudeness constituted a malicious, unjust accusation, a slander, and he humbly requested permission to arrest him then and there.

The Frenchman expressed profound indignation, saying that he did not understand such base ingratitude, whereupon my stepfather passionately declared that any punishment—a court of justice, even another criminal prosecution—was preferable to the life he had been subjected to up to that time as a member of the landowner's orchestra, which he would have left sooner but for his extreme poverty. With these words he left the room in the custody of the man who had arrested him. He was locked up in a remote room of the house and told that he would be sent into town the following day.

About midnight the door to the prisoner's room was opened. The landowner, carrying a lamp, entered in his dressing gown and slippers. It seemed that he could not sleep. A tormenting anxiety compelled him to leave his bed at that late hour. Yefimov, who also was unable to sleep, looked up at him in surprise. The landowner was profoundly disturbed. He set down the lamp and seated himself in a chair facing the bed.

"Yegor," he said, "why have you wronged me in this way?"

Yefimov did not reply.

The landowner repeated the question, and his voice vibrated with deep emotion and a curious anquish.

"God knows why I have wronged you, sir!" said my stepfather at last with a gesture of despair. "Must be some devil has led me astray! I don't know myself who put me up to it. . . . Well, it's no life for me there with you, it's no life. . . . The devil himself has got into me. . . . "

"Yegor," began the landowner once more, "come back to me; I'm willing to forget everything and forgive you. Listen, you'll be the first among my musicians, I'll pay you far more than the others——"

8

"No, sir, no, and don't even say it. I don't belong there with you! I tell you, the devil's got into me. I'll set fire to your house if I remain; a feeling of such despair comes over me sometimes that it would be better if I had never been born! I can't answer for myself just now; better leave me alone, sir. . . . It all started when I took up with that fiend."

"Who?" asked the landowner.

"Oh, the one that died like a dog, that Godforsaken Italian."

"Was it he, Yegorushka, who taught you to play?"

"Yes! He taught me plenty—to my ruin. I'd be better off if I'd never set eyes on him."

"Was he really a skilled violinist, Yegorushka?"

"No, he didn't know much, but he could teach. I really taught myself, he only showed me—but better my hand had withered away than to have this knowledge. Now I don't know myself what I want. Here, you ask me, sir: 'Yegorka, what do you want? I can give you everything.' And you see, sir, I can't say a word in reply, because I don't know myself what I want. No, I tell you again, you'd better leave me alone. I'd probably go and do something so you'd have to send me far away, and that would be the end of it."

"Yegor, I won't leave you like this," said the landowner after a momentary pause. "If you don't want to work for me, then go; you're a free man, I can't hold you back; but I won't leave you like this now. . . . Play something for me on your violin, Yegor, play for me, play, for God's sake! I am not ordering you, understand, I am not forcing you to play. I'm begging you with tears in my eyes: play for me, Yegorushka, for God's sake, play what you played for the Frenchman! Do this for me. . . . You're being obstinate and I'm being obstinate; it seems I have a stubborn streak too, Yegorushka! I understand you, but you must understand how it is with me too. I won't be able to live till you play for me, play of your own free will, what you played for the Frenchman."

"Well, so be it!" said Yefimov. "I made a solemn promise never to play for you, *especially* not for you, but now my heart has relented. I'll play for you, but this will be the first and last time, and then, sir, you will never hear me play again, never anywhere, though you were to offer me a thousand rubles."

And he took up his violin and began to play his own variations on a Russian song. B told me that this set of variations was his first and best piece for the violin, and that he never again played anything as well or with such inspiration. The landowner, who in any case could not listen to music without being moved, broke into sobs. When the piece was over he stood up and took out three hundred rubles, which he gave to my stepfather, saying:

"Now, go, Yegor. I'm releasing you, and I'll straighten out everything with the Count. But listen to me: let us not meet again. A broad road lies before you, and should we ever run into each other it would be painful for us both. And now, good-bye! . . . Wait! I have just one word of advice for you before you go, just one: don't drink—study, keep studying; and don't grow conceited! I'm speaking to you like a father. Take care, I repeat: study and keep away from the bottle—once you start drinking out of sorrow, and there'll be plenty of it—you're as good as finished, everything will go to the devil, and you too might end up in a ditch somewhere, like that Italian friend of yours. Well, good-bye! . . . Wait, kiss me!"

They embraced, and then my stepfather was set free.

He no sooner found himself at liberty than he set about squandering his three hundred rubles in the nearest town, where he had fallen in with a most disreputable and unsavory company of profligates. This ended in his being destitute and alone, without any means of support, and he was forced to join the miserable orchestra of an itinerant provincial theater as its first—and perhaps only—violinist. All this hardly conformed with his original intention of going to Petersburg as soon as possible to study, obtain a place in a good orchestra, and develop himself as an artist. But he was unable to reconcile himself to being a member of a small orchestra and soon quarreled with the manager of the theater and left. Then he became completely despondent and resolved on a desperate measure, one that was deeply mortifying to his pride. He wrote a letter to the landowner describing his situation and asking for money. The letter was written in a somewhat independent tone and failed to elicit an answer. He wrote a second letter, filled with the most obsequious expressions, calling the landowner his benefactor, extolling him as a genuine connoisseur of art, and again begging for help. At last an answer came. The landowner sent him a hundred rubles with a few lines in his valet's handwriting asking that in the future he be spared all such requests.

It had been my stepfather's intention on receiving the money to set out at once for Petersburg, but after paying his debts there was so little left that the journey was out of the question. Again he remained in the provinces, and again joined a provincial orchestra, but, as before, he was unable to get along in the company. He went on in this way, moving from place to place, always with the idea that he would manage to get to Petersburg before long, until he had spent six whole years in the provinces. At last he succumbed to a kind of terror. He had become desperately aware of how his talent, constantly impeded as it was by his wretched, disordered existence, was dwindling away. One morning he took his violin and set out for Petersburg, abandoning the theater manager and all but begging alms to get there.

He settled in a garret somewhere in Petersburg, and it was there that he first met B, who had just come from Germany and also planned to make a career for himself. They soon formed a friendship, which B recalls with deep feeling even to this day. Both were young, both had the same hopes and aspirations. But B was still in his early youth. Thus far he had experienced little suffering or want. He was essentially a German, moreover, and methodically and perseveringly strove toward his goal, fully conscious of his own powers and virtually counting on his success in advance; whereas his companion was already thirty, already tired and worn out, his patience exhausted and his youthful health and vigor dissipated in the exertions of earning a living during those years of playing in one provincial theater or landowner's orchestra after another. He had been sustained by a single, fixed idea: to get out of the odious position he was in, to accumulate some money, and go to Petersburg. But this had been a vague, obscure idea, a kind of irresistible inner impulse, which with the years had lost its original clarity even for Yefimov himself.

When he first arrived in Petersburg, he had acted almost unconsciously out of an ingrained habit of perpetually contemplating and wishing for that journey, almost as if he himself did not know what he was supposed to do in the capital. His enthusiasm, now somewhat jaundiced, was impetuous and erratic, as if he were trying to deceive himself, to persuade himself that his early energy, inspiration, and fire had not burned out. These endless transports impressed the cold, methodical B; he was dazzled by them, and hailed my stepfather as the great musical genius of the future. It was the only fate he could envisage for his friend.

But B's eyes were soon opened, and he saw through my stepfather completely. He clearly perceived that all his impetuosity, impatience, and feverish haste amounted to nothing but an unconscious despair at the recollection of his lost talent; that in the final analysis perhaps the talent itself had not been so great even in the beginning; that much of it was blindness, an innate complacency and feckless self-satisfaction that derived from endless fantasies and dreams about his own genius.

"And yet," B later confided to me, "I could not help marveling at the strange nature of my companion. I saw before me the desperate, feverish struggle between a convulsively strained will and an inner impotence. During those unfortunate years he had so gratified himself with dreams of future fame that he had failed to notice that he was losing what was most fundamental to our art and was forfeiting even the most elementary mechanics of the craft. Meanwhile, he was continually creating colossal plans for the future in his disordered imagination.

"And he not only wanted to be an outstanding genius, one of the foremost violinists in the world—indeed, already regarded himself as such—but he also thought of becoming a composer, although he knew nothing about counterpoint. But what surprised me most," added B, "was that this man, with his utter weakness and exceedingly superficial knowledge of the technique of music, had such a deep, such a clear, and one might even say instinctive understanding of the art. He felt it so intensely and had such an innate comprehension of it that it is not surprising that he mistook himself for a genius, for the high priest of art instead of a penetrating and instinctive critic. At times, in crude, simple language, he succeeded in revealing to me such deep truths that I was at a loss to understand how, without ever having read anything or studied with anyone, he was able to arrive at such conclusions, and my own development owed a great deal to him and to his advice.

"As far as I was concerned," B continued, "I was quite sanguine about myself. I too loved my art passionately, but I knew when I embarked on this course that I was not greatly gifted, that, properly speaking, I would be only a journeyman artist; yet I pride myself on not having hidden in the earth, like the slothful servant, the talent given to me by nature, but rather having increased it a hundredfold. If they praise the clarity of my playing and admire the precision of my technique, I owe it to ceaseless, indefatigable work, a clear awareness of my own powers, a tendency to self-depreciation, and an inveterate antipathy to overconfidence and the laziness that is the natural consequence of such complacency."

B tried in turn to counsel his friend, to whom he had subordinated himself in the beginning, but it only angered Yefimov and to no avail. This resulted in a coolness between them. B soon noticed that his companion was more and more frequently overcome by apathy, boredom, and despondency, and that his outbursts of enthusiasm became increasingly rare, all of which resulted in a grim, savage depression. At last Yefimov began to neglect his violin, sometimes not touching it for weeks on end. He was not far from complete degradation, and before long the poor man succumbed to all sorts of vice. And exactly what the landowner had warned him against happened: he abandoned himself to drink. B watched him in horror; his advice had no effect whatever, and he was afraid to utter a word of reproach. Gradually Yefimov was reduced to the most egregious cynicism. He had not the slightest compunction about living at B's expense and even acted as though he had a perfect right to do so.

Meanwhile their resources had been exhausted. B somehow made both ends meet by giving lessons and hiring himself out to play at evening parties given by merchants, Germans, and penurious government clerks who paid, if not well, at least something. Yefimov chose not to notice his friend's poverty; he treated him coldly and sometimes would not condescend to speak a word to him for weeks on end.

One day B remarked to him in the mildest possible tone that it might be better if he were a little less neglectful of his violin so as not to lose his skill with the instrument altogether;

whereupon Yefimov became absolutely furious, declaring that he had no intention of ever touching the violin again—as though he imagined that someone might go down on his knees and beg him to play.

The next time B needed a colleague to play with him at an evening party, he asked Yefimov to join him. The proposal threw Yefimov into a rage. He vehemently declared that he was no street musician, that unlike B, he would never sink so low as to debase a noble art by playing for vulgar artisans who were incapable of appreciating his skill and his talent. B made no reply, but after he had gone to fulfill the engagement, Yefimov, having reflected on his suggestion, decided that the whole thing had been nothing more than an allusion to the fact that he was living off B and the wish to let him know that he too ought to try to make some money. When B returned, Yefimov suddenly began to reproach him for the meannesss of his behavior and announced that he would not remain with him an instant longer. And, in fact, he disappeared for two days, but turned up again on the third day as if nothing had happened and resumed his old way of life.

Only his former friendship and attachment, not to mention the compassion he felt for a man who was destroying himself, prevented B from carrying out his intention of parting from him forever and putting an end to such an appalling existence. Ultimately they did part. Fortune smiled on B: he acquired a powerful patron and succeeded in giving a brilliant concert. By this time he had become a fine artist, and his rapidly growing fame earned him a place in the orchestra of the opera theater, where he soon won the success he fully deserved. On parting from Yefimov, he gave him some money and, with tears in his eyes, implored him to return to his true path.

Even now B cannot think of him without special emotion. His friendship for Yefimov had been one of the deepest experiences of his youth. They had begun their careers together, had formed an ardent attachment to each other, and, what was even more curious, Yefimov's most flagrant, obdurate short-comings had bound B to him more closely. B understood him; he saw through him and had a presentiment of how it would all end. On parting, they wept and embraced each other. Yefimov broke down and tearfully declared that he was a lost, unfortu-nate man, that he had known it for a long time, but only at that moment had he clearly perceived his ruin.

"I have no talent!" he said at last, turning pale as a corpse.

B was deeply moved.

"Listen, Yegor Petrovich," he said to him, "what are you doing to yourself? You are destroying yourself with despair; you have neither fortitude nor courage. In a fit of depression you now say you are without talent. It's not true! You do have talent, believe me! I see it, if only in your understanding and feeling for the art. I can show you how your whole life is proof of it.

"You have told me about your former existence—even then you were afflicted by the same sort of depression, though you may not have been aware of it. Then your first teacher, that strange man you told me so much about, awakened in you for the first time a love for art, and he recognized your talent. This feeling you have was just as intense and distressing then as now. But you yourself did not know what was happening to you. You couldn't go on living in that landowner's house, yet you didn't know what you wanted. Your teacher died too soon. You were left with nothing but vague aspirations and, what is more important, you had not been taught to understand yourself. You felt that you wanted to take another road, a broader one, that you were meant for a different fate, but you did not know how this was to be accomplished, and in your anguish, you felt an abhorrence for everything around you. Your six years of

16

poverty and misery were not lived in vain. You were learning, thinking, becoming aware of yourself and of your powers. Now you understand art and your own vocation.

"My friend, you must have patience and courage. A fate more enviable than mine awaits you: as an artist you are a hundred times greater than I, but may God give you even a tenth part of my endurance! Study, don't drink, as your good landowner said to you, but above all, begin anew—start with the rudiments. . . . What is it that torments you—poverty and privation? But poverty and privation form the artist. They are inseparable from the very beginning. Although nobody wants you now, nobody is even interested in you, the day will come.

"Wait, it will be quite different when they learn that you have talent. The envy, petty meanness, and, worst of all, the stupidity, will be far more galling to you than poverty. Talent needs sympathy, understanding, and you'll soon find out what sort of people will flock around you when you have even partly attained your goal. What you have developed through arduous work, sleepless nights, deprivation and hunger, they will deem worthless and regard with contempt. They will not acclaim you, will not comfort you, those future friends of yours; they will not point out what is good and true in you, but will take a malicious delight in pouncing on every mistake and pointing out exactly what is wrong with you, where you have erred, and, under the guise of indifference and disdain, will revel in every single thing you do wrong—as if anyone were without faults!

"But you are proud, and your arrogance, which is often uncalled for, may offend some egotistic nonentity; and then there will be trouble: you will be but one, and they will be many; you will be tormented by their pinpricks. Even I am beginning to experience this. But now you must take heart! You are not absolutely destitute, you'll be able to get along, only don't spurn humble work: go out and chop wood, which is what I did by playing at those artisans' parties. But you are impatient, it's a sickness with you. You lack simplicity; you're always scheming, thinking, too much goes on in your head. You're very bold when it comes to words, but you lose courage when it comes to taking up your violin. You are proud, but you lack fortitude. Have courage, have patience, and study; and if you can't trust your own powers, trust your luck; you have fire and feeling. Perhaps you will reach your goal; if not, trust your luck anyway: you won't lose in either case, for the gain is so great. That, my friend, is our *luck*—that the work is so great!"

Yefimov listened to his former comrade with deep emotion. As B talked, Yefimov's face lost its pallor and became flushed with animation, and his eyes sparkled with the unaccustomed ardor of hope and resolution. But this splendid courage soon changed to self-assurance, then to his usual insolence, and by the time B had reached the end of his exhortation, Yefimov had grown restive and was listening with wandering attention. He shook B's hand warmly, however, thanked him, and, always quick in his transitions from deep depression and self-abasement to extreme arrogance and defiance, confidently announced that his friend need not concern himself on his account as he was quite capable of arranging his own life, that he expected to have a patron before long and intended to give a concert, which would immediately bring him fame and fortune.

B shrugged his shoulders but did not contradict his former friend, and they parted, but, of course, not for long. Yefimov lost no time in squandering the money he had been given and came back a second, a third, and a fourth time, but by the tenth visit B's patience was exhausted and he was not at home to him. After that he lost touch with him altogether.

One day several years later, B was walking down a side street on his way home from a rehearsal when in the doorway of a filthy tavern, he stumbled on a drunken, shabbily-dressed man who addressed him by name. It was Yefimov. He was very much changed; his face had grown sallow and puffy, and it was obvious that a dissolute life had left its indelible mark on him. B was overjoyed to see him, and they had scarcely exchanged two words when he found himself being drawn into the tavern by Yefimov. There in a dingy little back room he examined his friend more closely. Yefimov was virtually in rags, his shoes down at the heel and his false shirt front rumpled and wine-stained. His graying hair had begun to fall out.

"How are things with you? What are you doing now?" asked B.

Yefimov was abashed, even cowed at first, and his answers were so disjointed and incoherent that B thought he was dealing with a lunatic. At last Yefimov confessed that he could not talk unless he had some vodka, but that they would no longer give him credit at the tavern. He flushed as he spoke and tried to hearten himself with a jaunty gesture, but what resulted was something so forced, so brazenly importunate that it was pitiful and aroused the sympathy of the kindhearted B, who saw that his fears had been fully justified. Nevertheless, he ordered the vodka. An expression of gratitude transformed Yefimov's face, and he was so flustered that tears came to his eyes and he was ready to kiss his benefactor's hands.

At dinner B learned to his great surprise that the unfortunate man had married. He was still more astonished when Yefimov told him that his wife was the source of all his misery and misfortune and that the marriage had completely destroyed his talent.

"How can that be?" asked B.

"My friend, I haven't touched the violin in two years," replied Yefimov. "She's a peasant, a cook, a coarse, uneducated woman. Damn her! . . . We do nothing but quarrel."

"But then why did you marry her?"

"I was starving when I met her; she had about a thousand rubles, so I rushed headlong into matrimony. And she was in love with me—hanging on my neck. Who wished her on me! Now the money's all gone, spent on drink, and as for my talent—finished!"

B noticed that for some reason Yefimov was anxious to vindicate himself in his friend's eyes.

"I've given it all up," he added.

Then he asserted that not long ago he had almost perfected himself as a violinist and that although B was one of the foremost violinists in the city, he could not hold a candle to him if he tried.

"Then what is the matter?" asked B, in surprise. "You should have found a place for yourself."

"It's not worth it!" said Yefimov, dismissing the question with a wave of the hand. "Who among you understands the least thing? What do you know? Nothing—that's what you know, absolutely nothing! You can scrape away at a dance tune for some ballet—that's your job. But you've never seen or heard a real violinist. Why exert yourself? Stay the way you are, that's what you want."

Yefimov again gesticulated, swaying drunkenly on his chair. Later he invited B to go home with him but B declined, took his address, and promised to drop in the next day.

By this time Yefimov had eaten his fill and, with mocking glances at his former friend, was making every effort to wound him. When they got up to leave, he snatched up B's handsome fur coat and helped him on with it like a subordinate toadying to his superior. As they passed through the front room of the tavern, he stopped and introduced B to the tavernkeeper and his patrons as the foremost, the one and only violinist in the whole capital. In short, his behavior on this occasion was thoroughly obnoxious.

Nevertheless B sought him out the next morning in the garret where we were living in extreme poverty, all in one room. I was four years old at the time, and my mother had been married to Yefimov for two years.

My mother was an unfortunate woman. She had formerly been a governess and was well-educated and attractive, but because she was poor had married my father, an elderly government functionary. She had been living with him only a year when he suddenly died. The meager inheritance was divided among several heirs, and my mother found herself left alone with me and only the trifling sum of money that fell to her share. To become a governess again with a small child on her hands would not have been easy. It was then that she happened to meet Yefimov, and fell genuinely in love with him.

She was an enthusiast and a dreamer; she saw in Yefimov some sort of genius, and believed his vainglorious talk of a brilliant future. The glamorous fate of being the guide and support of a man of genius appealed to her imagination, and she married him. All her hopes and dreams were dispelled in the first month, and she was left with only the woeful reality.

Yefimov, who may well have married my mother for her thousand rubles, sat back once the money was spent and, as if glad of an excuse, proceeded to announce to one and all that marriage had destroyed his talent, that it was impossible to work in a stuffy room with a hungry family before his eyes, that it was hardly the place to find inspiration for his music, and that such bad luck was obviously his destiny. Ultimately, he himself seems to have been persuaded of the validity of his grievances and was delighted at having this fresh pretext. It would appear that the unfortunate man, having betrayed his talent, was seeking some external circumstance to which he could attribute all his adversity and failure. He could not bring himself to accept the dreadful thought that he had long since been irretrievably lost to art. He struggled sporadically with this appalling conviction as with a harrowing nightmare, and when, from time to time, reality overpowered him and his eyes were opened, he was so horrified that he felt he was on the verge of losing his mind. He could not easily dissuade himself from what had for so long comprised his entire life, and continued to his last hour to think that his time had not yet passed. In his moments of doubt he abandoned himself to drink, and the distorting vapors of alcohol dispelled his anguish. Indeed, it is possible that he himself did not realize how necessary his wife was to him at the time. In her he had a living pretext, and he was genuinely obsessed by the idea that after he had buried his wife, *who had destroyed his talent,* all would go well as a matter of course.

My poor mother did not understand him. Like a true dreamer, she could not endure even the initial step into a hostile reality, and became bitter, irascible, and quarrelsome. She was almost always in conflict with her husband, who seemed to take pleasure in tormenting her, and she never ceased goading him to work. But my stepfather's fixed idea, his blindness and irrational behavior, made him insensitive and almost inhuman. He only laughed and swore that he would not touch the violin till his wife was dead, which he asserted with brutal candor even to her. Such an existence was unbearable for my mother, who continued to love him passionately to her dying day in spite of everything. She lived in perpetual torment, became chronically ill, chronically miserable, and, in addition to all her other woes, found herself the sole support of the family.

She had begun by preparing meals at home to be taken out. But her husband furtively stole from her any money she earned, and she was often obliged to send back empty dishes to her customers instead of the meals they had ordered. At the time of B's first visit, she had started taking in washing and dyeing old clothes. By such means we managed to live from hand to mouth.

B was shocked at our poverty.

"See here," he said to my stepfather, "what you were saying is nonsense! How could she have destroyed your talent? Why, she's supporting you! . . . And what are you doing?"

"Well, nothing," replied my stepfather.

But B was not yet aware of the full extent of my mother's misfortunes. Often her husband brought home with him a whole gang of ruffians and buffoons, and then there were frightful scenes!

B tried to reason with his former companion for some time. Finally he declared that he would give him no help whatever unless he was willing to reform, and told him in plain words that he would not give him money, as he would only spend it on drink. Then he asked him to play something on the violin so that he could see what might be done for him.

When my stepfather went out of the room to get his violin, B tried to give my mother some money, but she refused to take it. Then he gave it to me, and the poor woman shed bitter tears: it was the first time she had ever had to accept charity.

My stepfather came back with his violin, but said he would have to have some vodka before he could play. The vodka was sent for, and after taking a drink he became expansive.

"I'll play you something of my own, out of friendship," he said to B as he pulled a thick, dustcovered notebook out from under the bed.

"I composed all this myself," he said, pointing to the notebook. "This, my friend, is none of your rubbishy ballet music!"

B examined several pages in silence, then unrolled some sheets of music he had brought with him and asked my stepfather to play them instead of his own compositions.

My stepfather was rather offended, but fearing to lose his new patron consented to do as he was told. B saw at once that his old friend really had done a great deal of work since they had parted, and had improved despite his talk of not having touched the violin since his marriage.

My poor mother's joy was a sight to behold! She gazed at her husband with renewed pride. The kindhearted B, sincerely delighted, decided to get work for my stepfather. By then he had acquired important connections and lost no time in making inquiries and recommending his impoverished friend, having first exacted a promise that he would be on his good behavior.

He first bought him some decent clothes, then took him to see certain well-known persons on whom he counted to obtain work for him. Yefimov's boasting proved to be mere words, and he was only too glad to accept his old friend's proposal. B told me how embarrassed he had been by the abject deference and flattery with which my stepfather, in his fear of losing his patronage, had tried to keep in his good graces.

Realizing that he had been set on the right path, Yefimov even gave up drinking for a while. At last a place was found for him in a theater orchestra. He stood the test very well; by dint of application and hard work he regained in one month all he had lost in a year and a half of idleness, and promised that in future he would be conscientious and meticulous in fulfilling his duties.

But our family situation was in no way ameliorated. My stepfather did not give my mother a single kopeck of his salary, but spent it all on eating and drinking with the new friends he had rapidly acquired. For the most part he consorted with those who were associated with the theater in some minor capacity, such as chorus singers and dancers, in other words, with those to whom he felt superior, and avoided men of real talent. He managed to inspire in them a certain respect, immediately impressing upon them that he was an unrecognized genius, that his wife had ruined him, and that their orchestra conductor understood nothing about music. He derided all the other members of the orchestra, the selection of plays that were produced, and even the composers of the operas presented. Eventually he began to discuss some new theory of music. In short, he grew bored with the orchestra, quarreled with his colleagues and the conductor, was rude to his superiors, and acquired the reputation of being the most contentious, the most troublesome, and at the same time the most worthless of men. It finally reached a point where everyone found him intolerable. And, indeed, it must have been exceedingly odd to see in so indifferent a musician, in so poor and ineffectual a performer, such egregious pretensions, such boasting and self-conceit, and such an altogether insufferable manner. Having concocted and put into circulation some extremely malicious gossip, a positively scurrilous slander, he ended by quarreling with B as well.

After six months of unsatisfactory service in the orchestra, he was discharged for drunkenness and laxness in the performance of his duties. But he was not anxious to relinquish his position and soon turned up again in his old threadbare clothes, every decent article of clothing having been sold or pawned, and began going about with his former colleagues, regardless of whether or not he was welcome. He spread gossip, babbled nonsense, wept over his lot in life, and invited them all to come home with him and see for themselves what an abominable wife he had.

He found a ready audience among those who took pleasure in plying a former colleague with drink and leading him on to expound all sorts of absurdities. Besides, he generally expressed himself with a certain cleverness and wit, peppering his speech with cynical quips and caustic bitterness that delighted that type of listener. He was accepted as a crackbrained buffoon whose chatter was sometimes amusing to listen to if one had nothing better to do. They liked to provoke him by talking of some new violinist who was expected to appear. On hearing them, Yefimov immediately looked crestfallen and alarmed, tried to find out who the man was, how talented he might be, and was devoured by jealousy.

It seems that only at that time did his real, systematic insanity begin—his fixed idea that he was the foremost violinist, in Petersburg at any rate, but that he was a victim of fate, had been wronged, and, as a result of various intrigues, was misunderstood and unrecognized. This latter notion was actually gratifying to him, for there are those individuals who enjoy feeling wronged and oppressed, who like to complain of it audibly, or to console themselves in secret, glorying in their own unrecognized greatness. He could name every violinist in Petersburg, and to his mind there was not one who was his equal. Connoisseurs and dilettantes who were acquainted with the unfortunate lunatic liked to discuss in his presence some famous, gifted violinist in order to provoke his reaction. They enjoyed his malice, his apt acrimonious remarks, his clever criticism of the playing of his so-called rivals. Often they did not understand him, yet they were convinced that no one in the world knew so well how to caricature contemporary musical celebrities with his acuteness and audacity. The artists he ridiculed were somewhat afraid of him because they knew how caustic he could be, and recognized the pertinence of his attacks and the validity of his judgments in those cases where censure was merited. People grew accustomed to seeing him backstage and in the corridors of the theater, where he was allowed free access as if he belonged there, and he became a sort of local Thersites.

This way of life continued for two or three years, but at last he grew bored with it and with the role he had been playing.

Eventually he was barred from the theater officially, and in the last two years of his life apparently dropped out of sight and was no longer seen in his former haunts.

B happened to encounter him on two occasions, however, and Yefimov cut such a pitiful figure that again compassion prevailed over disgust. B hailed him, but my stepfather, who felt mortified, pretended not to hear him, and pulling his battered old hat down over his eyes passed him by.

Some time later, on the morning of one of the important holidays, B was informed that a former colleague of his, Yefimov, had come to offer his felicitations. B went out to him. Yefimov was drunk and began bowing very low to him, almost to the ground. His lips moved slightly as he stubbornly refused to enter the room, as if to imply: "And why should we untalented people consort with such notables as you? It's enough for us small fry to play the lackey, to offer our compliments, and then get out!" Apparently it was all very sordid, stupid, and grossly offensive.

After that episode B did not see him for a long time, in fact, not until the catastrophe that brought to an end that sad, disturbed, morbid life. It was terminated in a dreadful way. The catastrophe is closely connected not only with my childhood impressions, but with my whole life. This is how it happened. ... But first I must explain what my childhood was like, and what this man had meant to me who had such a grievous effect on my early life and was the cause of my mother's death.

TWO

My memories about myself go back only to the time when I was eight or nine years old. I do not know why, but all that had happened to me before then left no very clear impression that I can recall. But from the age of eight and a half I remember everything, day by day, as clearly as if it had happened yesterday. And yet there is something even earlier that I can remember as in a dream: a little lamp burning constantly in a dark corner before an ancient icon; my being knocked down in the street by a horse and, as I was told later, lying ill for three months as a consequence; how during this illness, on waking up at night in my mother's bed, frightened by morbid dreams, the silence of the night, and the scratching of mice in the corner, I huddled under the blanket by her side and trembled all night without daring to wake her—from which I conclude that I was more afraid of her than of any sort of terror.

But from the time I became aware of myself, I developed at a surprising rate, and many emotions that were by no means childlike were for some reason terribly accessible to me. Everything seemed to become clear and comprehensible with extraordinary rapidity. The period when I first began to understand myself left a bitter, melancholy impression on me. This impression, repeated day after day with increasing effect, cast a strange, dark shadow over the entire time I lived with my parents—over my whole life in fact.

In retrospect, it seems to me that I suddenly awoke as from a deep sleep, though it was not so marked at the time, of course. I woke up in a large, low-ceilinged room that was musty and unclean. The walls were painted a dingy gray color and there was an enormous Russian stove in one corner. The windows, long narrow slits, looked onto the street, or rather onto the roof of the house opposite, and the windowsills were so high above the floor that I remember having to put a bench or chair under them in order to reach the window, where I loved to sit when no one was at home. Half the city could be seen from our room, for we lived directly under the roof in a huge house. Our furniture consisted of nothing but a dilapidated, dusty, oilcoth-covered sofa from which the stuffing was falling out, an ordinary white table and two chairs, my mother's bed, a little cupboard that stood in one corner, a rickety dresser, and a torn paper screen.

It was dusk, I recall. Everything was scattered about the room in disorder: rags, brushes, our wooden dishes, a broken bottle, and what more I do not know. I remember that my mother was extremely upset and crying about something. My stepfather sat in the corner in his familiar tattered coat. He replied to something she had said with a smirk that made her still more angry, and then the dishes and brushes began to fly. I burst into tears and ran to them screaming. I was dreadfully frightened and clung to Father, trying to shield him with my body. Goodness knows why I thought that Mother was unjustly angry with him and that he was not to blame. I felt like begging forgiveness for him and enduring any punishment whatever in his place. I was terribly afraid of Mother and supposed that everyone else feared her too. At first she was astonished at what I had done, then she grabbed me by the arm and dragged me behind the screen. My arm struck the bedstead and was quite badly bruised, but my fear was even greater than the pain and I did not so much as wince.

I also remember Mother pointing to me and passionately and bitterly saying something to Father (I shall call him Father from now on, as I learned only much later that he was not related to me). This scene lasted for about two hours, and I was quivering with anxiety the whole time, wondering how it would all end. At last their quarrel subsided and Mother went out.

When she had gone, Father called me to him, stroked my head and kissed me, then took me on his knee. I nestled contentedly in his arms. That was perhaps the first parental caress I had ever known, and it may well have been the cause of my remembering everything so clearly from that time. I had also noticed that by standing up for him I had won Father's favor, and it was then that the idea first occurred to me that he had a great deal to put up with and suffered grievously because of Mother. This idea remained with me ever after, and my indignation increased with every day.

From that moment I began to feel a boundless love for Father, but it was a peculiar love, and by no means childlike; I should rather say it was some sort of compassionate, *maternal* feeling, if such a characterization were not a little absurd for a child's love. Father always appeared to me so very pitiful, so unbearably persecuted, so crushed and tormented, that it would have seemed dreadful and unnatural for me not to love him passionately, to caress him, comfort him, and do all I could for him. But to this day I do not understand exactly why I conceived the notion that he was such a martyr and the most unfortunate man in the world. Who could have suggested it to me? How could I, a mere child, have understood anything about his personal misfortunes? Yet I understood them, if in my own way, distorting and transforming them in my imagination. But even now I have no idea how I formed such an impression. Perhaps Mother was too severe with me and I became attached to Father as to someone who to my mind was a fellow sufferer.

I have described my earliest awakening from an infantile dream, my first impulse in life. My heart was vulnerable from the first, and my development was inconceivably forced and premature. From that moment I was no longer satisfied with external impressions. I began to observe, to think, to reason; but this observation began so unnaturally early that my imagination was constrained to transform everything in its own way, and I suddenly found myself living in a world of my own. Everything around me began to resemble the fairy tale that Father often related to me and which I readily accepted as the absolute truth. This engendered some very odd notions. I clearly perceived—though I do not know how this came about—that I belonged to a strange family, that my parents were not at all like any of the other people I happened to see at that time. "Why is it," I wondered, "that my parents don't seem to resemble other people, even in appearance? Why do I notice smiling faces elsewhere, while here in our garret room there is never any laughter or enjoyment?"

What power, what reason, compelled me, a nine-year-old child, to scrutinize people so intently, to listen to every word spoken by those I happened to meet on our staircase or in the street when in the evening, having covered my rags with Mother's old jacket, I went out to buy a few kopecks' worth of bread or sugar? I realized, but do not recall how, that there was some sort of permanent, unbearable sorrow in our home. I racked my brains trying to understand why this was so, and I do not know who may have helped me to unravel it all in my own way. I blamed Mother, regarded her as the bane of Father's existence, but again I say: I cannot understand how my imagination could have conceived such a monstrous idea. And the more attached I became to Father, the more I hated my poor mother. Even now the memory of all this is a poignant, bitter torment to me.

But there was another incident which, even more than the first, contributed to my strange closeness to Father. One evening at about ten o'clock, when he was not at home, Mother sent me out to buy yeast. On the way back I fell down in the street and spilled the whole cupful. My first thought was of how angry Mother would be. Then I suddenly felt a severe pain in my left arm and could not get up. Passers-by had stopped and gathered around me, and as an old woman helped me up, a boy running by struck me on the head with his fist. At last they got me to my feet and I picked up the broken fragments of the cup and staggered off, barely able to move my legs. All at once I caught sight of Father. He was standing in a crowd in front of the magnificent house directly opposite ours, which belonged to an illustrious family. The house was splendidly illuminated, scores of carriages were drawing up to the entrance, and music floated through the open windows. I tugged at Father's coat-tails, showed him the broken cup, and, bursting into tears, told him I was afraid to go home to Mother. For some reason, I was confident that he would stand up for me. But why was I confident of this? Who had suggested it to me? Who had made me believe that he loved me more than he loved my Mother? Why did I turn to him without fear?

He took my hand and comforted me, then told me he wanted to show me something and lifted me up in his arms. But I was unable to see anything because he had clasped my injured arm and I was in severe pain. I did not cry out, however, as I was afraid of annoying him. He kept asking me whether I could see anything. I tried my best to give him an answer that would please him, and said that I saw some crimson curtains. But when he wanted to carry me to the other side of the street, nearer to our house, I suddenly began to cry, clinging to him and begging him to hurry and take me up to Mother. I remember that all at once Father's endearments distressed me, that it seemed to me unbearable that one of the two people whom I wanted so much to love was tender and loving to me, while the other intimidated me so that I dared not go back to her. . . . But Mother was hardly angry at all and simply sent me to bed. I remember that the pain in my arm grew increasingly worse till I became feverish. Even so, I was singularly happy because everything had turned out well, and I dreamed all night of the house with the crimson curtains.

When I woke up the next morning, my first concern, my very first thought, was for the house with the crimson curtains. Mother was hardly out of the house before I scrambled up to the little window and looked out at it. This house had aroused my childish curiosity in the past. I enjoyed looking at it, especially toward evening when the streetlamps were lighted, and when the crimson, almost magenta-colored curtains began to glow with a blood-red flame behind the great windowpanes of the brilliantly illuminated house. Sumptuous carriages drawn by handsome, spirited horses were continually driving up, and the commotion of their arrival, and the resplendent ladies who came in them, excited my curiosity. In my childish imagination all this assumed the aspect of a regal pageant or an enthralling fairy tale. But after my encounter with Father in front of this magnificent house, it became doubly interesting and alluring to me, and my inflamed imagination gave rise to wondrous fancies and conjectures. It is hardly surprising that I became such a strange, fantastic child, living as I did with people as strange as my mother and father.

I became acutely aware of their contrasting characters. I was struck, for instance, by the fact that Mother was incessantly bustling about and fretting over our pitiful household, and forever reproaching Father because she alone toiled for the family, and I could not help wondering why he did absolutely nothing to help her, why he lived like a stranger in our home.

From certain things she said I formed a vague notion about it: I learned to my surprise that Father was an artist (the word stuck in my mind), that he was a man of talent, and my imagination instantly formed a concept of an artist as a special sort of person, unlike other men. Perhaps it was Father's behavior that led me to this conclusion; perhaps I had once heard something that remained in my memory; certainly I had been singularly impressed by a remark I had once heard him make with intense feeling. What he had said was: "The time will come when I will not be living in poverty, when I'll be rich, and a gentleman. I'll be born anew when *she* dies."

I remember being desperately frightened by this. I could not remain in the room but ran out into our chilly vestibule, where I leaned on the windowsill, buried my face in my hands, and sobbed. Then, after thinking it over and becoming reconciled to Father's dreadful wish, fantasy suddenly came to my aid. I could not go on torturing myself with uncertainty and had of necessity to arrive at some sort of conclusion. And so I finally told myself—and I do not know exactly how all this began—that when Mother died Father would leave our dismal garret and take me away with him. But where? (Even until quite recently I found this hard to visualize.) I only remember that everything with which I could adorn the place to which I would go with him—and I was certain that we would go together—everything beautiful and magnificent that my fantasy could possibly devise, animated those dreams. It seemed to me that we would become rich at once, and that I would no longer be sent on errands, which had always distressed me because the children next door invariably tormented me every time I went out of the house. And I was in particular dread of this when fetching milk or oil, knowing that if I spilled it I would be severely punished. Then, still dreaming, I decided that Father would order fine clothes for himself, and that we would move into a beautiful house. Here the magnificent house with the crimson curtains and my encounter there with Father came to the aid of my imagination. And it followed directly in these dreams that we would move into that very house and live there in some kind of perpetual holiday and eternal bliss. From then on I spent the evenings at the window gazing with intense curiosity at that, to me, enchanted dwelling, and I remembered all the guests who arrived, attired with an elegance such as I had never seen before, and imagined that I heard the strains of sweet music floating through the windows. I peered at shadowy figures glimpsed behind curtained windows, trying to guess what they were doing there, and it all seemed like paradise to me, like an eternal holiday.

I loathed our wretched lodging and the rags I had to wear, and one day when Mother shouted at me, ordering me to leave the window where I had perched as usual, the thought instantly flashed into my mind that she did not want me to look at that house or even to think about it, because our happiness displeased her and this was her way of thwarting it. All that evening I observed her with intent, suspicious eyes.

What could have engendered such cruelty in me, and toward such a perpetually unhappy creature as my mother? Only now do I understand her life of tribulation and cannot think without anguish of that harassed woman. Yet even then, in the dark period of my strange childhood, that period of unnatural development in my early life, my heart was often wrung with pity, and this anxiety, doubt, and confusion left their imprint on my mind. And even then I felt pangs of conscience and suffered remorse over the injustice of my mother's life. But for some reason we were strangers to each other, and I cannot remember that I ever expressed any affection for her. Now sometimes the most insignificant memories wound and trouble my soul.

I remember once (of course, what I now relate is trivial, elementary, and of no importance, but it is just such memories that have particularly tormented me and are most painfully lodged in my memory), on a certain evening when Father was not at home and Mother was about to send me out to buy sugar, that she kept changing her mind, and, counting over the coppers, the pitiful sum at her disposal, was unable to come to a decision. I believe that she counted them aloud for half an hour, and still could not work out her calculations. Besides, at certain moments, probably out of sorrow, she lapsed into a kind of vacuity. As I now recall, she kept repeating something, counting in a low, monotonous voice, and the words seemed to fall from her lips of themselves. Her cheeks and lips were white, her hands trembled, and she shook her head as always when deliberating in private.

"No, we don't need it," she said, glancing at me. "I'd better go to bed. . . . Well? Are you sleepy, Netochka?"

When I did not answer, she lifted my head and gazed down at me with such a sweet, tender look, and her face lit up with such a luminous, maternal smile, that my heart was rent and throbbed with emotion. She had called me Netochka, moreover, which meant that she specially loved me at that moment. It was a name she herself had coined, affectionately changing my name, Anna, to the diminutive Netochka, and when she called me by that name, it meant that she felt tenderly toward me. I was so moved that I wanted to embrace her, to cling to her, to weep with her.

She, poor thing, continued to stroke my head for a long time; perhaps she had forgotten what she was doing and kept it up mechanically as she repeated again and again: "My child, Anneta, Netochka!" I could hardly restrain my tears but was determined to control myself. For some reason I was obdurate and refused to show my feelings, though I was torturing myself.

36

This cruelty could not have been natural to me; this alienation could have been caused only by her severity. . . . No! I had been corrupted by my fantastic, exclusive love for my stepfather.

I used to wake up in the night, huddled under the cold blanket on my little pallet in the corner, always frightened of something. Half-asleep, I would recall how not so long ago, when I was smaller, I had slept in Mother's bed, and then I was not so scared when I woke up at night; I had only to press close to her, shut my eyes and clasp her tightly, and I would fall asleep again. And I still felt that somehow I could not help secretly loving her. Later in life I observed that many children are monstrously unfeeling, and when they love someone, love him to the exclusion of all others. So it was with me.

There was often a deathlike silence in our garret room for weeks on end. When Father and Mother grew weary of quarreling, life reverted to what it had been before, and I was silent, thoughtful, always melancholy, and always seeking for something in dreams. As I observed them both, I fully understood their relation to each other; I understood the perpetual, smoldering hostility they felt toward one another, understood all the grief and perturbation with which life in our disordered home was fraught. Of course, I understood it only to the degree possible for me at the time, and not its causes and effects. Sometimes during the long winter evenings, forgotten in my corner, I watched them intently, scrutinizing Father's face in a constant effort to divine his thoughts and discover what it was that preoccupied him.

At times I was startled and alarmed by Mother. Often she would pace tirelessly to and fro for hours at a time; sometimes even in the middle of the night when she could not sleep she would get up and walk about the room, whispering to herself as if she were alone, now throwing up her hands, now clasping them to her bosom, now wringing them in terrible, inexhaustible anguish. And the tears streamed down her face, tears which perhaps she herself did not understand, since she lapsed into a state of oblivion from time to time. She was suffering from a serious illness, which she completely neglected. And I remember that my solitude, and the silence which I dared not break, became more and more oppressive to me.

For a whole year I had been living a very conscious life, always thinking, dreaming, and secretly tormented by the vague, mysterious desires that had suddenly sprung up in me. I was as tremulous as a woodland creature. And then one day Father took notice of me for the first time, called me to him, and asked me why I was looking at him so intently. I do not recall my answer; I only remember that he grew thoughtful and at last looked at me and said that the next day he would bring home a primer and start teaching me to read. I looked forward with impatience to this primer and dreamed of it all night without clearly understanding what it was. The following day he really did begin to teach me. I was quick to grasp what was required of me, and became an apt and ready pupil, knowing that this would please him. Those were the happiest moments of my life at that time. And when he praised me for my intelligence and kissed me, I wept for joy.

Little by little Father grew fond of me, and before long I ventured to talk to him. We often talked for hours on end, though there were times when nothing he said was comprehensible to me. But I was somewhat afraid of him, afraid he might think I found it dull being with him, so I did my best to make him believe that I understood everything. Before long, sitting down with me in the evening had become a habit with him. As soon as it began to grow dark, he returned home and I went to him with my primer. He made me sit on a little stool facing him, and when the lesson was over he always read to me from a little book. Although I did not understand what he read, I kept laughing gleefully, thinking it would please him. And seeing me laugh did in fact amuse him and he became more cheerful.

One day after the lesson he told me a fairy tale. It was the first fairy tale I had ever heard. I listened to him spellbound, following every word with burning impatience. I was transported to another world, and by the end of the story was in a state of ecstasy. But it was not the story itself that produced this effect on me—no, it was that I supposed it to be true, and, giving free rein to my exuberant fantasy, immediately confused reality and fiction. In my imagination I saw the house with the crimson curtains. Then Father appeared as one of the characters in the story—how I do not know, since it was he who was relating it to me—and Mother too was in it, hindering Father and me from going away somewhere together. And at last, or perhaps I should say from the first, with my extravagant imagination, my strange dreams filled with weird, improbable phantoms, all this became so confused in my mind that it produced utter chaos, and for a certain time I lost all judgment, all sense of the present, of reality, and God knows where I was living.

All during this time I was longing to talk to Father about what awaited us in the future, about what he was planning to do, and where he would take me when at last we quit our attic room. I was absolutely confident that this would happen soon, but how it would happen and what form it would take I did not know and only tortured myself by racking my brains over it. Sometimes—and this generally occurred in the evening—I felt that at any moment Father would surreptitiously wink at me, call me into the vestibule, and that I would snatch up my primer and our one picture—the grimy lithograph devoid of frame that had hung on our wall from time immemorial, and which I had firmly resolved to take with me—and we would run away, never to return home to Mother.

One day when Mother was out I chose a moment when Father was particularly genial—which happened only when he had not drunk too much—and started talking to him with the intention of turning the conversation to the cherished subject. When I had succeeded in making him laugh, I threw my arms around his neck, and with my heart throbbing as though I were about to speak of something awesome and mysterious, and growing more and more muddled and incoherent as I went along, I began questioning him about where we were going, whether we would leave soon, what we would take with us, how we would live, and, finally, whether we were going to live in the house with the crimson curtains.

"What house? Crimson curtains? What is this? What are you babbling about, silly child?"

Then, with still greater trepidation, I tried to explain to him that when Mother was dead he and I would no longer live in the garret, that he would take me away and we would be rich and happy, and I ended by assuring him that all this he himself had promised me. And in trying to convince him, I completely convinced myself that he actually had spoken of all this before.

"Your mother? Dead? When your mother is dead . . .?" he repeated, knitting his thick, grizzled eyebrows as he looked at me in amazement. "What are you talking about, you poor, stupid child?"

Then he began to scold me, telling me over and over again that I was a silly baby, that I did not know anything, and I do not recall what more; I only remember that he was exceedingly annoyed.

I did not understand one word of his reproaches, nor did I realize how painful it was for him to learn that I had overheard things he had said to Mother in rage and deep despair, that they had impressed themselves on my mind and had been given a great deal of thought. Whatever he himself was like at the time, however extravagant his own mania, all this quite naturally shocked him. And though I had no idea why he was angry, I was nonetheless terribly hurt and unhappy and began to cry. It had seemed to me that all that lay ahead of us was so momentous that I, a stupid child, had hardly dared contemplate it, much less speak of it, before. And, despite my inability to understand him, I had dimly sensed from the very first word that in some way I had wronged Mother. I was assailed by fear and horror, and doubts began to creep into my soul. Then, seeing that I was suffering and in tears, he began to comfort me, dried my tears on his sleeve, and told me not to cry. We both sat in silence for some time, he frowning and apparently thinking about something. After a while he began talking to me, but no matter how I strained my attention, I could not understand what he was saying.

From certain scraps of this conversation which I remember to this day, I conclude that he must have been trying to explain to me who he was, that he was a man of tremendous talent, a great artist, whom nobody understood. I also remember that after asking me whether I understood him and, of course, being given a satisfactory answer, he made me repeat it: Was he talented? Yes, he was talented. He smiled slightly at my reply; perhaps in the end he himself saw the absurdity of discussing with me what was to him such a serious subject.

Our conversation was interrupted by the arrival of Karl Fyodorych, and I was at once diverted and burst into merry laughter when Father pointed to him and said:

"Now, you take Karl Fyodorych here—he hasn't got a particle of talent."

This Karl Fyodorych was a most amusing person. There were so few people in my life at that time that I could not possibly forget him. I can see him now: he was a German by the name of Meyer, who had left his native country and come to Russia out of a burning desire to join the Petersburg ballet company. But he was such an inferior dancer that he was not accepted even for the corps de ballet, and had been employed as a supernumerary in the theater. He played various bit parts such as one of the soldiers in the suite of Fortinbras, or one of the twenty-odd noblemen of Verona who raise their pasteboard poniards in unison and cry: "We will die for the King!" Yet there was probably not another actor in the world as passionately dedicated to his roles as he was. The greatest calamity and disappointment of his life was that he had failed to get into the ballet company. To him the art of ballet surpassed all other arts, and he was as wedded to it in his way as was Father to the violin.

The two men had become acquainted when both were still employed in the theater, and from then on the retired supernumerary never forsook my stepfather. They met frequently and commiserated with each other over their hard lot and lack of recognition. The German was the most sensitive, most devoted of men, and the friendship he bore my stepfather was fervent and selfless; but it seems that Father was not particularly attached to him and only suffered his companionship for want of anyone else. It was unthinkable to Father, moreover, that ballet should be regarded as an art, and this reduced the poor German to tears. Knowing his sore spot, Father always attacked it, and when poor Karl Fyodorych flew into a passion trying to prove his point, he only made fun of him.

I later heard more about him from B, who called him "the Nuremberg upstart." B told me a great deal about Karl Fyodorych's friendship with Father, and among other things how time and again when they had been drinking together they would start bewailing their fate and lack of recognition. I remember these occasions, and also remember that watching those two eccentric men I too used to fall into a fit of whining without knowing why. This only happened in Mother's absence. The German was dreadfully afraid of her and always stood in the hall waiting for someone to go out so he could find out whether or not she was at home, and if she was, he instantly ran downstairs.

He invariably brought some German poetry with him and became feverishly excited when he read it aloud to Father and me; then he would translate it for our benefit and declaim it in his broken Russian. This amused Father immensely, and I sometimes laughed till tears came to my eyes.

One day they got hold of a Russian work that roused them both to such a pitch of excitement that from then on they reread it almost every time they met. I recall that it was a drama in verse by some famous Russian writer. The opening lines became so fixed in my mind that years later, when I happened to come across the book, I had no difficulty in recognizing it.

This drama dealt with the misfortunes of a certain great painter, one Gennaro or Jacobo, who on one page cried: "I am unrecognized!" and on the next: "I am recognized!" or: "I am untalented!" and a few lines later: "I am talented!" And it all ended most lamentably. It was, of course, an exceedingly commonplace work, but the amazing thing was the naive and tragic way in which both readers, who found in its hero a great similarity to themselves, reacted to it.

I recall that there were times when Karl Fyodorych became so impassioned that he sprang up and rushed across the room to Father and me (whom he called *Mademoiselle*) to beg and implore us with tears in his eyes then and there to be the arbiter of his fate, to judge between him and the public. Whereupon he would commence to dance, calling out to us as he executed various steps to tell him instantly what sort of dancer he was,

43

whether he was an artist or not, and whether one could possibly say otherwise.

Father was always highly entertained by this and would covertly wink at me as if expecting to enjoy a good laugh at the German's expense. I thought it terribly funny, and though I was choking with laughter tried to restrain myself at an admonitory gesture from Father. Even now, I cannot help laughing just thinking about it. I can still see poor Karl Fyodorych: extremely short, very thin, already graying, and with a red, tobacco-stained, hooked nose and monstrously crooked legs—of which he must nonetheless have been proud, as he wore very close-fitting trousers.

I remember him making a final leap and taking a pose with arms outstretched, smiling as dancers on the stage smile at the end of the last figure. Father remained silent for several moments as though unable to bring himself to pronounce judgment, deliberately leaving the "unrecognized" dancer to hold his position on one foot, swaying from side to side as he did his utmost to maintain his balance. At last Father looked at me solemnly, as if inviting me to be an impartial witness to his pronouncement; meanwhile, the dancer had fixed his timid, imploring gaze on me.

"No, Karl Fyodorych, you'll never make it!" said Father at last, feigning a reluctance to speak the bitter truth.

Whereupon Karl Fyodorych uttered a heartfelt moan, but instantly rallied and with fleeting gestures again requested our attention, assuring us that his method had been wrong before, and beseeched us to judge him once more. And running to the other end of the room he leapt into the air with such fervor that he struck his head against the ceiling and got a nasty bruise. But be bore the pain like a Spartan, again assumed a ballet pose at the end, again smiled and extended his quivering arms to us, and again begged us to decide his fate. But Father was inexorable, and, as before, dolefully announced:

"No, Karl Fyodorych, it's obviously your fate—you'll never make it."

At that point I could no longer contain myself and burst into laughter, as did Father after me. Karl Fyodorych at last saw that we were making fun of him. He flushed with indignation, and with tears in his eyes and deep if somewhat ludicrous emotion (which later made me feel very remorseful), said to Father:

"You are a treacherous friend!"

And snatching up his hat he fled, vowing never to return.

But these quarrels were of short duration; within a few days he would again appear in our lodgings, again start reading the famous drama, and again the tears flowed and the naive Karl Fyodorych begged us to be the arbiter of his fate, imploring us this time to judge him seriously, as true friends, and not to mock him.

One day I was returning home from the store where Mother had sent me to buy something, carefully holding the change in my hand, when I met Father coming downstairs on his way out. Unable to contain my joy on seeing him, I broke into a laugh, and as he bent down to kiss me, he noticed the coins in my hand. . . . I have forgotten to say that I knew every expression of his face so well that I could perceive his least wish at a glance. When he was melancholy I was torn with anguish. What vexed him most frequently and most intensely was having no money and, as a consequence, being unable to get a drop to drink. But at that moment, when I encountered him on the stairs, I felt that something unusual was taking place within him. His eyes were dull, his gaze shifted evasively, and at first he failed to notice me; but when he caught sight of the gleaming coins in my hand he suddenly flushed, turned pale, started to extend his hand to take the money away from me, then quickly withdrew it. He was obviously undergoing an inner struggle. At last he seemed to take hold of himself and told me to go upstairs. After descending several steps he stopped abruptly and called me to him.

"Listen, Netochka," he said, "give me that money, I'll return it to you. All right? You'll give it to Papa, won't you? You're a good little girl, aren't you, Netochka?"

It was as though I had had a presentiment that this would happen. The first thing that flashed into my mind was how angry Mother would be; my timidity, and, still more, my instinctive shame both for myself and for Father, kept me from giving him the money. He instantly perceived this and hastened to say:

"Oh, never mind, never mind . . . "

"No—, Papa, take it. I'll say I lost it, that the children next door took it away from me."

"Well, all right, all right. You see, I knew you were a clever little girl," he said, his lips quivering as he smiled at me, and no longer concealing his delight when he felt the money in his hand. "You're a good girl, you're my little angel! Now, let me kiss your little hand."

He took my hand and was about to kiss it, but I quickly withdrew it and, though a feeling of compassion came over me, I was beginning to be still more tormented by shame. I ran upstairs in dismay, leaving Father without saying good-bye to him.

When I entered our garret room, my cheeks were burning and my heart beat with an oppressive sensation that I had never known before. Nevertheless, I resolutely told Mother that I had dropped the money in the snow and had been unable to find it. I expected a whipping at the very least, but this did not happen. At first Mother was really beside herself with grief, because we were desperately poor. She started shouting at me, then seemed to think better of it and left off scolding, saying only that I was a clumsy, careless child, and that evidently I did not love her very much if I could not take better care of her money. This remark hurt me more than if she had whipped me. Mother understood me very well. She was aware of my sensitivity, which often reached a point of morbid irritability, and knew that to reproach me for lack of love would make a deeper impression on me than any punishment and force me to be more careful in future.

At dusk, when it was time for Father to come home, I went to the vestibule to wait for him as usual. I was terribly disturbed. My emotional state was exacerbated by agonizing pangs of conscience. At last Father returned and I was over-joyed at his arrival, as if I thought it would bring me relief. He was in high spirits from drink, but on seeing me instantly assumed a troubled, mysterious air, drew me into a corner, and with an apprehensive glance at our door took out of his pocket a piece of gingerbread he had bought and in a whisper began to enjoin me never to dare take money and hide it from Mother, that this was bad, shameful, very wrong; that it had been done this time because Papa was very much in need of the money, but he would return it, and later I could say I had found it; but to take money from Mamma was shameful and I should never again even think of doing such a thing, and if I obeyed him in this he would buy more gingerbread for me. He even went so far as to add that I ought to feel sorry for Mamma, that she was such a pitiful, sick woman, and it was she alone who worked for us all.

I listened to him in consternation, my whole body trembling and my eyes brimming with tears. I was so shocked that I could not utter a word or move from where I stood. At last, after telling me not to cry and not to say anything about this to Mother, he went into our room. I noticed that he too was terribly perturbed.

I was so appalled by what had happened that I could not

look at Father and for the first time did not go near him all evening. I felt that he was avoiding my eyes too. Mother paced the room in her usual abstracted state. She was worse that day, having had some sort of attack. Eventually, as a result of my mental anguish, I became feverish. That night I was unable to sleep. I was tormented by morbid dreams. When I could no longer bear it, I began to weep bitterly. My sobs woke Mother and she called to me, asking me what was the matter. I did not answer but cried still more bitterly. She lit a candle, came to me and tried to soothe me, thinking I had been frightened by a dream.

"Oh, you silly little girl," she said, "still crying at your age because of something you've dreamed. Now, now, that's enough. ... "

Then she kissed me and told me to come and sleep in her bed. But I refused; I could not bring myself to go with her or to put my arms around her.

I was racked by unimaginable tortures. I wanted to tell her everything, and was on the verge of doing so when the thought of Father and his admonitions stopped me.

"Oh, Netochka, you poor little thing!" said Mother, tucking me into bed and wrapping her old cloak around me when she saw that I was shivering. "You're probably going to be ill, just like me."

And she gazed at me so sorrowfully that I could not bear her look and shut my eyes and turned away.

I do not remember falling asleep, but for a long time, while still in a doze, I heard Mother coaxing me to go to sleep. I had never before undergone such excruciating torment. I was heart-stricken.

The next morning I felt better. I talked to Father, but made no mention of the previous day, surmising that this would please him. He brightened up at once, though till that moment he had scowled every time he glanced at me. Now a sort of joy, an almost childish pleasure, took possession of him at the sight of my cheerful face. Soon Mother went out, and then he could not restrain himself. He began kissing me till I was in a state of almost hysterical ecstasy, laughing and crying at the same time. Finally he said that because I was such a good, clever little girl he was going to show me something very beautiful, something I would be delighted to see. Whereupon he unbuttoned his waistcoat and took out a key that hung from his neck on a black cord. Looking mysteriously into my eyes as if wanting to see in them all the pleasure which, in his opinion, I ought to feel, he opened the trunk and carefully took from it a curiously shaped black case which till that moment I never knew he had. He lifted the case with a kind of veneration, and seemed to be completely transformed; there was no longer a trace of mockery in his face, which all at once had assumed a rather solemn expression. He opened the mysterious case with the key and took from it an object I had never seen before. Carefully and reverently holding it in his hands, he told me that it was a violin—his instrument. Then he began talking volubly in a low, solemn voice, but I did not understand what he was saying, and all that remained in my memory were certain phrases which were already known to me: that he was an artist, that he was talented, that sometime in the future he would play the violin, and that eventually we would be rich and attain great happiness. The tears welled up in his eyes and streamed down his face. I was deeply moved. At last he kissed the violin and gave it to me to kiss. Seeing that I wanted to examine it more closely, he led me to Mother's bed and placed the violin in my hands, but I noticed that he was trembling all over for fear that I might break it. I held the violin in my hands and touched the strings, which gave out a faint sound.

"That's music!" I said, glancing up at Father.

49

"Yes, yes, music!" he repeated, rubbing his hands together exultantly. "You're a clever child, you're a good child!"

For all his commendation and delight I could see that he was uneasy about his violin, and I too became fearful and made haste to hand it back to him.

The violin was returned to its case with the same care, the case was locked and put into the trunk and, after stroking my head once more, Father promised that every time I was a good, clever, obedient girl he would show me his violin.

And so the violin dispelled our mutual misery. Only in the evening, as he was going out, Father whispered to me that I should not forget what he had said to me the day before.

And thus I was growing up in our garret room, and gradually my love—no, I might better say my passion, though I do not know a word strong enough fully to convey the unbridled, tormenting feelings I had for my stepfather—reached a kind of morbid perversity. I had but one pleasure: to think and dream about him; but one desire: to do anything that might give him the least gratification. How many times I used to stand at the staircase waiting for his return, frequently shivering and blue with cold, only that I might know of his arrival an instant earlier and set eyes on him that much sooner. I was practically delirious with joy whenever he happened to caress me even casually. And at the same time I was often agonizingly distressed by my obdurate coldness toward poor Mother. There were moments when, just looking at her, I felt torn by pity and anguish.

I could not be indifferent to their constant animosity and felt that I had to choose between them, and had to take somebody's side, and I took the side of that half-mad being solely because in my eyes he was so pitiful and abject, and because he had so unaccountably excited my fantasy from the very first. But who knows? Perhaps I became attached to him precisely because he was so strange, even in appearance, and because he was not so solemn and morose as Mother; because he was virtually mad and often displayed a sort of buffoonery, a sort of childishness; because I feared him less, and even respected him less than Mother. He was somehow more my equal. And gradually I had come to feel that I was actually above him and had to some extent subjugated him, had even become necessary to him. I was secretly proud of this and exulted in it. I understood why I was necessary to him and at times coquetted with him.

This strange attachment of mine was really more or less like a romance. . . . But the romance was not destined to go on very long: I was soon bereft of both Father and Mother. Life ended for them both in a terrible catastrophe, which is grievously, poignantly fixed in my memory. This is how it came about. . . .

THREE

All Petersburg was excited by the extraordinary news of the day. There was a rumor in circulation concerning the imminent arrival of the celebrated S___ts, and the entire musical world of Petersburg was agog. Singers, actors, poets, painters, music lovers, and even those who were not music lovers and unassumingly affirmed that they did not know a note of music, rushed with avid enthusiasm to obtain tickets. The hall could not hold one tenth of the devotees who were able to pay twenty-five rubles for admission. The European name S___ts, his laurel-crowned old age, the unfading freshness of his talent, the report that in recent years he had but rarely taken up his bow to gratify the public, and the certainty that this would be his last European tour before going into retirement, all combined to produce a total and profound impression.

I have already mentioned that the arrival of every new violinist, anyone with the least claim to fame, had a most unfortunate effect on my stepfather. He was always among the first to rush to hear the visiting artist in order to ascertain as quickly as possible the degree of his artistry. Often he became positively ill as a result of the resounding tributes paid to the recent arrival, and was only appeased when he could find defects in the new violinist's playing and spread his caustic judgments far and wide. The poor madman believed that there was but one talent, one artist, in the whole world, and that artist was, of course, himself. But word of the expected arrival of S___ts, a musical genius, had a shattering effect on him.

It must be observed that in the past ten years Petersburg had not heard a single celebrated genius who was even comparable to S___ts, consequently my stepfather had no concept of the playing of first-class European artists.

I was told that at the first mention of the violinist's appearance Father was again seen backstage at the theater. It was said that he appeared in an excited state and made nervous inquiries concerning S___ts and the forthcoming concert. He had not been seen in the theater for some time, and his appearance produced a certain effect. Someone who evidently wanted to provoke him turned to him and, with a challenging air, said:

"And now, my dear Yegor Petrovich, you won't be hearing ballet music, but something that will probably make your life not worth living."

They say he turned pale at the gibe and with a frenzied smile replied:

"We shall see: 'Reverence is greater from a distance.' After all, S___ts has probably just been in Paris, so it's the French who are shouting about him—and everyone knows what the French are!"

There was an outburst of laughter. The poor man felt affronted but controlled himself and added that he had nothing to say for the moment. "But we shall see, we'll soon find out. The day after tomorrow is not far off, and then we'll no longer have to wonder."

B tells how that same evening, before dusk, he encountered Prince Kh___y, the well-known dilettante, a man with a deep love and appreciation of art. As they walked on together, talking of the newly arrived artist, suddenly at a street corner, B caught sight of my stepfather standing in front of a shop, gazing intently at a handbill displayed in the window announcing the concert to be given by S___ts.

"Do you see that man?" said B, pointing to my father.

"Who is he?" asked the Prince.

"You've heard of him before. It's that same Yefimov I've spoken to you about several times, and to whom you have already extended your patronage."

"Oh, that curious fellow!" said the Prince. "You've told me plenty about him. They say he's very interesting. I'd like to hear him play."

"It's not worthwhile," responded B. "And it's very distressing. I don't know how it would affect you, but for me it's always heartrending. His life is dreadful, a hideous tragedy. I feel for him, deeply, and regardless of how low he has sunk I still feel sympathy for him. You say that he is curious, Prince. That is true, but he makes a terribly pitiful impression. First, he is mad; moreover, three crimes rest upon this madman, for he has not only destroyed himself but has ruined two other lives—those of his wife and daughter. I know him; he would die on the spot if he were made to realize what he has done. But the horror of it is that for eight years now he has been *almost* persuaded of it; for eight years he has been wrestling with his conscience in an effort to recognize it, not just partly, but fully."

"He is poor, you say?" inquired the Prince.

"Yes, but his poverty is in effect his happiness: it provides him with an excuse. Now he can assure everyone that it is only poverty that hinders him, and that if he were rich he would have more time, would be free of cares, and then they would see what an artist he is. He married with the singular expectation that a thousand rubles, which his wife had inherited, would help him to get on his feet. He behaved like a visionary, like a poet, but he's been acting like that all his life. Do you know what he has been asserting constantly for eight years? He insists that his wife is the cause of his poverty, that it is she who stands in his way. But take that wife away from him—and he would be the unhappiest man in the world.

"It is several years now since he has touched the violin, and do you know why? Because every time he picks up his bow he is forced to admit to himself that he is nothing—a cipher, not an artist. But when he has laid aside his bow, as he has done now, he at least has a remote hope that this is not true. He is a dreamer; he thinks that by some miracle he will suddenly, at a single stroke, become the most famous man in the world. His motto is: *Aut Caesar, aut nihil*—as if Caesar could have become what he was in the twinkling of an eye. He yearns for fame, but if that sort of feeling becomes the principal, the sole, incentive of the artist, the man is not an artist, because he has already lost the cardinal artistic instinct, that is, the love of art simply because it is art and not something else—not fame. Now S __ ts is the exact opposite: when he takes up his bow, nothing in the world exists for him except music. And after the violin, his main concern is money. Fame, I believe, comes only third, but he pays little heed to it.

"Do you know what now occupies this unfortunate man?" continued B, indicating Yefimov. "He is engrossed in the most fatuous, futile, the most pathetic and absurd question conceivable; namely, is he superior to S___ts or is S___ts superior to him—nothing less! And all because he is still convinced that he is the foremost musician in the world. Persuade him that he is not an artist and, believe me, he would die on the spot. He would be thunderstruck. It would be awful to deprive him of the fixed idea to which he has sacrificed his whole life, and which, in any case, is basically deep and serious, for in the beginning his claim was just."

"It will be interesting to see what happens to him when he hears S___ts," observed the Prince.

"Yes," B replied thoughtfully. "But, no, he will recover at

once; his madness is stronger than truth, and he will immediately concoct some sort of excuse."

"You think so?" asked the Prince.

By this time they had reached my father. He would have slipped by unnoticed, but B stopped him and started to talk to him. He asked him whether he intended to go to the concert. My father nonchalantly replied that he did not know, that he had a certain enterprise in hand that was of greater importance than any concert or passing virtuoso; he might consider it, however, he would see, and if he happened to have a free hour—why not? He might manage to get away for a while. Then, smiling uncertainly, he darted an anxious look at B and the Prince, clutched his hat, nodded, and walked off, giving the excuse that he was in a hurry.

I had been aware of Father's anxiety the day before. I did not know exactly what was troubling him, but I saw that he was terribly disturbed. Even Mother had noticed it, though she was quite ill at the time and barely able to get about. He had been coming and going continually. Three or four of his old companions had come to see him in the morning, which surprised me, as we never saw anyone but Karl Fyodorych, everyone else having given up visiting us after Father left the theater. Later in the day Karl Fyodorych rushed in, breathless with excitement, bringing a handbill announcing the concert. I listened to everything attentively, and as I watched them I became as perturbed as if I were to blame for all the agitation and anxiety I saw in Father's face. I was eager to understand what they were talking about; it was the first time I had heard the name S___ts. Afterward I understood that one had to have at least fifteen rubles in order to see this artist.

I also remember that Father could not restrain himself, and with a gesture of impatience declared that he knew all about those outlandish prodigies, those unheard-of talents, that he knew S___ts too, and it was always the Jews who tried to grab Russian money, because Russians, in their simplicity, would believe any sort of nonsense, especially anything the French started shouting about. . . . I already knew what the word *untalented* meant. The visitors had begun to laugh, and soon they all departed, leaving Father utterly disconsolate.

I realized that for some reason he was angry with this man S___ts, and to dispel his misery, and also to get into his good graces, I went to the table, took up the handbill, and began to decipher aloud the name S___ts. Then, laughing and looking around at Father, who sat in a chair sunk in thought, I said:

"He's probably just like Karl Fyodorych—he'll probably never make it either!"

Father started as if he had been frightened, and tore the handbill from my hand. Then, stamping his feet and shouting at me, he snatched up his hat and made for the door. Suddenly he turned, called me out to the vestibule and kissed me, telling me that I was a clever girl, a good child, that I surely did not want to upset him, and that he expected some great service of me—exactly what he did not say. It was very painful for me to listen to him; I felt that all he said, all his endearments, were insincere, and I was shaken by this. I began to be tormented with anxiety over him.

The next day at dinner—it was the day before the concert—Father seemed to be completely crushed. He was dreadfully changed and kept darting looks at both Mother and me. I was surprised when at last he started talking to her—surprised because he almost never spoke to her. After dinner he was unusually attentive to me, calling me out to the vestibule every minute or two on various pretexts, then glancing about as if fearful of being found there. He kept stroking my head and kissing me, saying that I was a good child, an obedient child, that I surely loved Papa and surely would do what he asked of me. All this became unbearably oppressive. Finally, when he had called me out for the tenth time, everything became clear to me. Glancing about with a nervous, distraught look, he asked me whether I knew where Mother had put the twenty-five rubles she had brought home the day before. I was horrified by the question. But just then a sound was heard on the stairs and Father, alarmed, rushed out of the house.

Toward evening he returned, troubled, melancholy, and distracted. He sat in his chair in silence, from time to time darting diffident glances at me. I was seized with dread and purposely avoided his eyes. Eventually Mother, who had remained in bed all day, called me to her, and, giving me a few copper coins, sent me out to buy her some tea and sugar. Tea was very rarely drunk in our house: Mother permitted herself to indulge in what, with our means, amounted to a luxury only when she felt ill and feverish.

I took the money, went out to the vestibule, and then started running as though afraid of being overtaken. But what I had foreseen happened: Father caught up with me in the street and led me back to the foot of the stairs.

"Netochka!" he began, his voice trembling. "My darling! Listen—give me that money, and tomorrow I'll—"

"Papa! Papa, dear!" I cried, falling to my knees and imploring him. "Papa, I can't! I mustn't! Mamma needs the tea. . . . I can't take it from Mamma, I simply cannot! Another time I'll get it for you. . . ."

"So you won't do it? You won't do it?" he whispered in a kind of frenzy. "So, that means you don't love me? All right, then! I'm going to leave you now. You can stay with Mamma. I'm going away, and I won't take you with me. Do you hear, you wicked girl? Do you hear?"

"Papa!" I screamed in horror. "Take the money—here! . . . Now what am I to do?" I sobbed, tugging at his coattails. "Mamma will cry. . . . Now she will scold me again!"

58

He evidently had not expected such resistance; nevertheless he took the money, and, unable to endure my sobbing and lamenting, left me on the stairs and rushed out. I went back upstairs, but at the door to our room my strength failed me: I could not go in, dared not go in. Every feeling in me was outraged, wounded. I covered my face with my hands and rushed to the window as I had done the first time I heard Father express a wish for Mother's death. I was in a sort of daze, benumbed and quaking as I listened for the least sound on the staircase. At last I heard someone hurriedly climbing the stairs. It was he; I recognized his step.

"You're here?" he asked in a whisper.

I ran to him.

"There!" he cried, thrusting the money into my hand. "There! Take it back! I am no longer your Father, do you hear? I don't want to be your Papa now! You love Mamma more than me, so go to Mamma! I never want to see you again!"

And he pushed me aside and ran downstairs again. I rushed after him weeping.

"Papa, dearest Papa! I'll obey you! I love you more than Mamma! Take the money—take it back!"

But he did not hear me; he had gone.

All that evening, crushed by grief, I shivered feverishly. I remember Mother saying something to me, calling me to her, but I was practically unconscious, unable to see or hear anything. This terminated in a fit of crying and screaming, and Mother was so alarmed she did not know what to do with me. She took me into her bed, but I cannot remember falling asleep, only that I clasped my arms around her neck and quivered with terror the whole night.

I woke up very late in the morning, after Mother had gone out. At that time she was always going out on some business of her own. A stranger had come to see Father and they were talking together in loud voices. I could hardly wait for the visitor to go, and the moment Father and I were alone I went to him sobbing and begging him to forgive me for what had happened the previous day.

"And will you be a clever little girl as you were before?" he asked me sternly.

"I will, Papa, I will!" I replied. "I'll tell you where Mamma keeps her money. She keeps it in that little drawer—it was there in the box yesterday."

"Where was it?" he cried, starting up from his chair. "Where?"

"It's locked up, Papa!" I said. "Wait till evening when Mamma sends me out for change; she will, because I saw that there were no more coppers left."

"I need fifteen rubles, Netochka! Do you hear? Only fifteen rubles! Get it for me today—I'll return it all tomorrow. And I'm going to buy you some sugar candies right now, and I'll buy you some nuts too . . . and a doll . . . and tomorrow too . . . and I'll bring you a present every day if you'll be a clever little girl."

"You don't have to, Papa, you don't have to! I don't want any candies—I won't eat them—I'll give them all back to you!" I cried, bursting into tears.

I was suddenly heart-stricken. I felt that he was merciless, that he did not love me, because he could not see how much I loved him and thought I was willing to do what he asked of me only for the sake of presents. At that moment I, a child, understood him through and through, and I felt that this realization had wounded me forever, that I could no longer love him, that my papa was lost to me.

He, however, was in a kind of ecstasy over my promise; he saw that I was ready to venture anything for him, would do anything he wished—and only God saw how great that "anything" was for me at that moment. I knew what the money meant to poor Mother, knew she might fall ill from the grief of losing it, and I was harrowed with remorse. But he saw nothing; he treated me like a three-year-old child, when, in fact, I understood everything. His rapture knew no bounds; he kissed me, prevailed upon me not to cry, and, no doubt appealing to my endless fantasies, promised that we would leave Mother and go away together that very day. In the end, having taken the concert handbill out of his pocket, he explained to me that the man he was going to see was his enemy, his mortal enemy, but that no enemy of his would prosper.

It was rather he who very decidedly resembled a child with his nonsensical talk about his enemies. When he at last noticed that I was listening to him in silence instead of smiling as I usually did when he talked to me, he took his hat and made haste to go out, kissing me once more before leaving, however, then cocking his head and smiling as if uncertain of me and trying to make sure that I would not change my mind.

I have already said that he was like a madman, but this had become still more apparent since the previous day. The money he needed was for a ticket to the concert, which was to resolve everything for him. He seemed to have had a premonition that this concert would decide his fate once and for all, but he was so distracted that on the preceding day he had tried to take a few coins away from me, as if that would have enabled him to buy the ticket. His strangeness betrayed itself still more at dinner. He was unable to sit still and did not touch his food but kept jumping up from the table and sitting down again as if he had just thought of something. At one moment he became strangely abstracted, muttering under his breath, and at the next began darting glances at me, winking and making signs as though impatient to get the money and vexed with me for not having got hold of it for him.

Even Mother noticed his odd behavior and gazed at him in amazement. I felt as though I were under a death sentence.

When dinner was over, I crouched in a corner, trembling feverishly and counting the minutes as I waited for the time when Mother usually sent me out to buy something. In my entire life I had never spent more agonizing hours; they will remain in my memory forever. What I lived through during that time! There are moments in one's life in which one consciously experiences far more than in whole years.

I felt that I was doing something wicked; he himself had encouraged my better instincts when, after faintheartedly prompting me to do wrong the first time, he had subsequently had misgivings and explained to me that what I had done was bad. Was it really possible that he could not understand how difficult it is to deceive an impressionable nature, one who at an early age had felt deeply and comprehended a great deal of good and evil? Yet I realized that it was obviously his desperation that had made him decide again to lead me into sin, thus sacrificing my poor defenseless childhood and once more throwing into confusion an unstable conscience.

And so, huddled in a corner, I brooded over all this. Why had he promised to reward me for what I had already decided to do of my own free will? New feelings, new longings, questions I had never thought of before, surged into my mind and tormented me. Then all at once I began to think about Mother; I visualized her distress at the loss of her last earnings.

At last she laid aside her work, which had exhausted her, and called me. I trembled as I went to her. She took some money out of the dresser and gave it to me saying:

"Go, now, Netochka. Only for God's sake, don't let them cheat you as they did the other day, and don't lose the money!"

I looked at Father beseechingly, but he only nodded and gave me an encouranging smile as he rubbed his hands together impatiently. The clock had just struck six and the concert was to begin at seven. He too had been under a great strain during those hours of suspense.

I stopped on the stairs and waited for him. He was so excited and impatient that he instantly abandoned all caution and ran out after me. I gave him the money; it was dark on the stairs and I could not see his face, but I felt that he was trembling all over as he took it from me. I stood there as if stunned, unable to move, and only recollected myself when he told me to go back upstairs and get him his hat. He did not want to go back himself.

"Papa! Won't you—won't you go with me?" I asked brokenly, thinking of my last hope, that he would intercede for me.

"No, you had better go alone. . . . Well?. . . Wait, wait!" he cried, as if suddenly thinking of something. "Wait now, I'm going to get you a present in just a minute, but first you go up and get my hat and bring it down here to me."

All at once my heart felt constricted, as if gripped by hands of ice. I screamed, pushed him away from me, and ran upstairs. When I went into our room I was as white as a sheet, and if at that moment I had tried to say that someone had taken the money away from me, Mother would have believed me. But I was incapable of uttering a word. In a paroxysm of despair, I flung myself down on Mother's bed and buried my face in my hands. A moment later the door creaked faintly and Father entered. He had come for his hat.

"Where is the money?" Mother shrieked, having guessed at once that something out of the ordinary had happened. "Where is the money? Tell me! Tell me!"

And she yanked me off the bed and stood me in the middle of the room.

I was speechless; my eyes were glued to the floor; I hardly knew what was happening or what was being done to me.

"Where is the money?" she cried once more, abruptly turning from me to Father, who had snatched up his hat. "Where is the money" she repeated. "Ha! So you've ruined her too! A child! Her—her!. . . Oh, no! You won't get away like that!"

She darted to the door in a flash, locked it from the inside, and took the key.

"Speak! Confess!" she said to me in a voice so choked with emotion that it was barely audible. "Confess everything! Tell me—you tell me or—or I don't know what I will do to you!"

She seized my hands, wringing them as she questioned me. She was in a frenzy. At that moment I vowed I would remain silent and not say a word about Father, and, in a final appeal, timidly raised my eyes to him. One glance from him, one word, some sign of what I had hoped and prayed for, and I would have been happy, regardless of the suffering and torment. . . . But, my God! with a heartless, threatening gesture he ordered me to be silent—as if at that moment anyone else's threat could have intimidated me. I felt choked, I could not breathe; my legs gave way and I fell to the floor unconscious. It was a recurrence of the previous day's nervous attack.

I came to at the sound of someone knocking at the door. When Mother opened it I saw a man in livery who surveyed us all in astonishment as he entered the room. He asked for the musician Yefimov. Father gave his name and the footman handed him a note which he said was from B, who at that moment was at the Prince's house. The envelope contained a ticket for the concert.

The appearance of a footman in sumptuous livery, giving the name of his master, the Prince, who had sent him expressly to the poverty-stricken musician Yefimov, all produced an instantaneous effect on my mother. I have mentioned earlier in describing her character that the poor woman still loved her husband. And now, after eight long years of ceaseless anguish and tribulation, her heart remained unchanged: she was still able to love him! God knows, perhaps she had suddenly envisaged a change in his fate. Even the shadow of a hope could influence her. How can one know—perhaps she had been infected with the unshakable self-confidence of her mad husband! Indeed, it is hardly possible that such self-confidence should have been entirely without influence on her, a weak woman, and at this attention from the Prince she was capable of instantaneously formulating thousands of plans for her husband. All at once she was ready to turn to him again, to forgive him for what he had made of her life, even in the light of his most recent crime—the sacrifice of her only child—and in a burst of renewed enthusiasm, a transport of renewed hope, to reduce the crime to a simple shortcoming, the pusillanimity induced by penury, his sordid existence and hopeless position. Enthusiasm was not dead in her, and at that moment she was again capable of forgiveness and an inexhaustible compassion for her ravaged husband.

Father had commenced to bustle about; he too was impressed by the attention of B and the Prince. He straightway turned to Mother and whispered something to her, after which she went out. She returned shortly with some money she had changed, and Father proceeded to give a silver ruble to the messenger, who bowed politely upon departing.

Meanwhile, Mother had again left the room; she came back with an iron and having taken out her husband's best shirt front began pressing it. She herself tied the white batiste necktie, which had been preserved in his wardrobe since time immemorial on the chance that it might be needed, together with the shabby black dress coat left from the days of his theater employment.

His toilet completed, Father took up his hat, but before leaving asked for a glass of water. He sank down in a chair, pale and completely exhausted. It was I who had to give him the water; feelings of hostility may have risen in Mother's heart again, dampening her enthusiasm.

Father went out and we were left alone. I huddled in a corner, silently observing Mother for a long time. I had never seen her so distraught: her lips quivered, her pale face suddenly flamed, and from time to time a shudder ran through her body. At last she gave vent to her anguish in stifled sobs and was soon wailing and lamenting.

"It is I—I who am to blame for everything, miserable woman that I am!" she said, talking to herself. "What will become of her? Whatever will become of her when I die?" she went on, standing stock-still in the middle of the room as if stunned by the thought. "Netochka, my child! Poor little thing! My unfortunate little girl!" she said, taking my hand and embracing me convulsively. "Who will take care of you when I am gone, if I am unable to bring you up, to care for you and watch over you even when I am alive? . . . Oh, you don't understand me! Can you understand? Will you remember? Will you remember what I am saying to you now, Netochka? Will you recall it in the future?"

"I will, I will, Mamma!" I said, clasping my hands beseechingly.

She held me in her arms for a long time, as if dreading the thought of being separated from me. My heart was ready to burst.

"Mamma, dear! Mamma!" I said, beginning to cry. "Why don't you . . . why don't you . . . love Papa?" And my sobs prevented me from continuing.

A deep moan escaped her. Then in the throes of deepest anguish she commenced pacing to and fro.

"My poor, poor child! And to think, I did not even notice how she was growing up! She knows, she knows everything! My God! What an impression, what an example!" And she wrung her hands in despair.

Later she came to me and kissed me in a frantic outburst of love, then kissed my hands, her tears falling on them as she implored my forgiveness. Never had I seen such suffering.

At last she was exhausted and seemed to fall into a doze. For a whole hour she did not stir. When she got up, weary and spent, she told me to go to bed.

I went to my corner and wrapped myself in a blanket, but I could not fall asleep. I was anxious about Mother, anxious about Father. I waited restlessly for his return. A feeling of dread came over me at the thought of him.

About a half hour later Mother came with a candle to see whether I was sleeping. To put her mind at rest, I shut my eyes and pretended to be asleep. After looking at me, she quietly went to the cupboard and poured herself a glass of wine. She drank it and went back to bed, leaving the candle burning on the table and the door unlocked, as always when Father was out late.

I lay there more or less in a doze, but sleep would not come. No sooner would I shut my eyes and begin to fall asleep than I woke up with a start from a ghastly dream. My anxiety grew more and more intense. I felt like screaming, but the scream died in my breast. At last, when it was quite late, I heard the door open. I do not recall how much time had elapsed, but when I really opened my eyes, I saw Father. He was sitting in a chair near the door and seemed to be sunk in thought. He looked dreadfully pale. There was a deathlike silence in the room. The guttering candle cast a dismal light over everything.

I watched him for a long time, but he did not move; he remained in the same position with his head down, his hands clenched on his knees. I wanted to call out to him but could not. My numbness persisted. Suddenly he roused himself, lifted his head, and got up from the chair. He stood in the middle of the room for a few moments as if trying to come to a decision about something; all at once he walked over to Mother's bed, and after listening to make sure that she was asleep, went to the trunk where he kept his violin. After unlocking it, he took out the black violin case and placed it on the table, then he again looked about him, but with a dim fugitive glance such as I had never before observed in him.

He was about to take up the violin when he suddenly left it to go and lock the door. Noticing the open cupboard, he very quietly went to it, saw the wine, poured himself a glass and drank it. Once again he was on the point of taking up the violin, but this time left it to approach Mother's bed. I was numb with fear as I waited to see what would happen.

He appeared to be listening to something for a long time, then all at once he threw back the blanket, uncovered her face, and felt it with his hand. I shuddered. He bent down again with his head quite close to her, and when he raised himself a smile seemed to flicker over his dreadfully pale face. He gently and carefully drew up the blanket, entirely covering the sleeping woman. I began to tremble with some unknown dread. I became fearful for Mother, fearful of her deep sleep, and I peered anxiously at that still, rigid form outlined under the blanket. . . . A horrifying thought flashed through my mind.

His preparations completed, Father went back to the cupboard and drank the rest of the wine. He was trembling all over as he approached the table. His face was so ashen that it was hardly recognizable. Again he took up the violin. I looked at it, knew what it was, only this time I expected something frightful, something ineffable and terrible, and I shuddered at the first note. Father began to play, but the sounds came somewhat spasmodically; he kept stopping momentarily, as if remembering something, and finally, with a distraught, tortured expression, he laid down the bow, and with a strange look turned toward the bed. Something there disturbed him, and again he went over to it. I did not miss a single move he made and was numb with fear as I watched him.

All at once he began hurriedly groping for something, and the same harrowing thought once more flashed through my mind. Why was Mother sleeping so soundly? Why had she not woken up when he touched her face? Then I saw that he was dragging out everything he could find, all of our clothing—Mother's old cloak, his old frockcoat, a dressing gown, even the dress I had taken off—and was covering her completely, concealing her under the heap of things he piled on her. She lay motionless, not even a hand stirred.

She was sleeping so deeply!

When he had finished his task, he seemed to sigh with relief. Nothing had hindered him in what he was doing, yet he appeared to be troubled about something. Moving the candle, he turned to face the door so that he could not see the bed. At last he took up the violin, and with an almost desperate gesture, struck the strings with the bow. And the music began.

But it was not music. . . . I remember everything distinctly, to the very last moment, everything that left me so aghast at the time. No, it was not music as I was later to know it. It was not like the sounds that came from a violin, but like some horrific voice resounding through our dismal lodgings for the first time. Either my impressions were false and morbid, or my senses, reeling from all I had witnessed, were prepared for terrifying sensations and endless torments; in any case, I was firmly convinced that I heard moans, cries, weeping; the sum of human despair poured out in those sounds, till at last, with the final, awesome chord in which there was all the horror of a lament, the agony of affliction, and the grief of hopeless despair, I could no longer endure it. I was trembling, tears streamed from my eyes, and with a terrified, desperate scream I rushed to Father and seized his arm. He uttered a cry and lowered the violin.

For a moment he was bewildered, then his eyes started out of his head and he looked about as if searching for something. Suddenly he raised the violin and brandished it over my head. . . . Another instant and he might have killed me outright.

"Papa!" I shrieked. "Papa!"

He trembled like a leaf when he heard my voice and fell back a step or two.

"Ah, so you're still left! So it's not all over! You're still here with me!" he cried, taking me by the shoulders and lifting me up.

"Papa!" I screamed once more. "Don't scare me, for God's sake! I'm so frightened! Aie!"

He was struck by my cry. Gently setting me down again he looked at me in silence for a moment as though recognizing or remembering something. Then an awful thought seemed to occur to him and he changed abruptly; the tears welled up in his bleary eyes and he leaned down and looked intently into my face.

"Papa!" I cried, racked by fear. "Don't look at me like that, Papa! Let's go away from here! Let's go away quickly!... Let us go—let us run away!"

"Yes, we'll run away, we'll run away! It's high time! Come, Netochka! Hurry, hurry!"

And he bustled about as if he had only just realized what he must do. Casting a swift glance over the room and seeing Mother's kerchief, he picked it up and put it in his pocket; then his eye fell on a nightcap and he picked that up too and stuffed it into his pocket, as if seizing on anything he thought might be needed for a long journey.

I slipped on my dress and also began snatching up whatever seemed to me necessary for the journey.

"Is that everything? Is that all?" asked Father. "All ready? Hurry, hurry!"

I hastily tied up the bundle, flung a kerchief over my head, and was about to leave when it suddenly occurred to me to take the picture that hung on the wall. Father unhesitatingly agreed. He had grown very quiet and spoke in a whisper, urging me to be quick. The picture hung very high on the wall: we had to place a little stool on top of a chair in order to reach it, and only after great difficulty were we able to get it down.

Then we were ready for our journey. Father took me by the hand and we were on our way out when he suddenly stopped. He stood rubbing his forehead for several minutes as if trying to recollect something that remained to be done. Eventually it seemed to have come to him that he had to find the key (which was under Mother's pillow), and he began hurriedly looking through the dresser. He found some money in a drawer and brought it to me.

"Here, take this, take good care of it!" he whispered. "Don't lose it now—remember, remember!"

First he put the money in my hand, then took it back and thrust it in the front of my dress. I remember that I shuddered when the silver touched my body, as if realizing only then what it was. Again we were about to go, and again he stopped me.

"Netochka!" he said, as if making a great effort to think. "My child, I forgot. . . . What is it? What did I want to do? . . . I can't remember. . . . Yes, yes! It's come to me, now I remember! Come here, Netochka!"

He led me to the corner where the icon was and told me to kneel.

"Pray, my child, pray! It will be better for you. . . . Yes, it really will be better," he whispered to me, pointing to the icon and looking at me strangely. "Pray, pray!" he said in an imploring voice.

I quickly knelt down and folded my hands in prayer, but I was so overcome with horror and despair that I fell to the floor and lay there for several minutes as if dead. I tried to concentrate all my thoughts and feelings in prayer, but was overcome by fear. I got up, exhausted by my anguish. I no longer wanted to go with him, I was afraid of him now; I wanted to remain where I was. Finally the thought that had been tormenting me exploded in a cry.

"Papa!" I said, the tears streaming down my face. "But . . . Mamma—what's the matter with Mamma? Where is she?. . Where is my Mamma?"

I could not go on and shed bitter tears.

He too was in tears as he looked at me. He took me by the hand and led me to the bed, swept aside the heap of clothing he had piled on it, and turned back the blanket. My God! She lay there dead, already grown cold and blue. I frantically flung myself on her and embraced her lifeless body.

"Bow down to her, child!" he said. "Say good-bye to her."

I bowed down as did Father. . . . He was dreadfully pale; his lips quivered as he whispered something.

"*It was not I,* Netochka, *not I,*" he said to me then, pointing to her body with a trembling hand. "Listen, *it was not I; I am not guilty of this.* Remember, Netochka!"

"Papa, let's go," I whispered in terror. "It's time."

"Yes, it's time, it has long been time," he said, taking me firmly by the hand, and we hastily left the room. "Well, now we set off! Thank God, thank God, now it is all over!"

We went downstairs; the porter, half-asleep, glanced at us suspiciously as he opened the gate, and Father, as if fearing to be questioned, slipped out ahead of me and I had difficulty catching up with him. We walked down our street and came out on the canal embankment. Snow had fallen during the night, covering the stone pavements, and was still drifting down in fine flakes. It was cold; I was chilled to the bone as I tagged after Father, clutching his coattails. He carried his violin under his arm, and from time to time stopped to shift it to a more secure position.

We had walked for about a quarter of an hour when he turned down an incline and sat on the curbstone at the edge of the canal. There was an ice hole only two feet from us; not a soul was in sight. God, how well I remember the frightening sensation that came over me all at once! What I had dreamed of for a whole year had at last come true. We had left our miserable garret. . . . But was it this that I had looked forward to and dreamed of? Was it this that my childish fantasy had created when I visualized that happiness of which I was enamored in a quite unchildlike way?

But above all at that moment I was tortured by the thought of Mother. Why had we left her, I wondered, abandoning her body like some unwanted thing? This, I recall, caused me more remorse and torment than anything else.

"Papa," I began, unable to endure my excruciating anxiety. "Papa!"

"What is it?" he asked sternly.

"Why did we leave Mamma there? Why have we forsaken her?" I asked, beginning to cry. "Papa! Let's go home! Let's go back and get someone to help her."

"Yes, yes!" he exclaimed with a start, springing up from the curbstone as if something had just occurred to him which resolved all his doubts. "Yes, Netochka, this is wrong. You must go back to Mother; she's cold there. Go to her, Netochka, go! It won't be dark—there's a candle in the room. Don't be afraid, go and call someone in for her, and then come back here to me. You go alone, I'll wait for you here. . . . I won't go away."

I set off at once, but I had no sooner reached the sidewalk than I suddenly felt as if something had pierced my heart. . . . I turned and saw that he had started running in the opposite direction, that he was running away from me, leaving me alone, abandoning me at that moment! I cried out with all the strength that was in me and rushed after him terror-stricken. But I was soon out of breath; he kept running faster and faster, and before long was out of sight. I came upon his hat, which he had lost in flight, picked it up, and started running again. But I was breathless and my legs were giving way. I felt as if something hideous was happening to me. I kept feeling it was a dream, and had the same sensation I had often experienced in dreams of running away from someone and having my legs fail me, of being overtaken by my pursuer and falling down unconscious.

Yet I was torn by an agonizing feeling of pity for him; my heart ached when I pictured him running away without coat or hat, and running away from me, from his beloved child. I wanted to catch up with him for this alone, to kiss him warmly once more and tell him not to be afraid, to set his mind at rest and be assured that I would not follow him if he did not want me to, but would go back to Mother by myself.

At last I saw him turning into another street. I ran there and turned in after him; I could still see him in the distance. . . . But then my strength gave out and I began crying and screaming. I remember that in my flight I had collided with two passers-by who stopped in the middle of the sidewalk and gazed at us both in amazement.

"Papa! Papa!" I screamed for the last time.

All at once I slipped on the sidewalk and fell down near the gates of a house. I felt as if my whole face was covered with blood. A moment later I lost consciousness.

74

I woke up in a warm, soft bed and saw beside me the kind and friendly faces of people who greeted my awakening with joy. There was an old woman with spectacles, a tall gentleman who gazed at me with deep compassion, a beautiful young lady, and an old gray-headed man who was holding my hand and looking at his watch.

I awoke to a new life. One of the men I had collided with on my flight was Prince Kh___y, and it was at the gates of his house that I had collapsed. After a prolonged investigation, they found out who I was, and the Prince, who happened to be the man who had sent Father the concert ticket, was so impressed by the singularity of the circumstances that he decided to take me into his home and bring me up with his own children. They tried to ascertain what had become of Father and learned that he had been apprehended in a fit of raving lunacy—by then he had reached the outskirts of the city—and taken to a hospital, where he died two days later.

His death was the natural consequence of all his life had been. He had to die when everything with which he sustained himself in life collapsed, dissolved like a phantom, like an empty, intangible dream. He died when his last hope had vanished, when everything with which he had deluded himself and buttressed his entire existence was seen for what it was. The unbearable illumination of truth blinded him, and what was false became false even for him.

In his last hour he had heard an extraordinary genius, and this had made clear to him what he himself was, and he stood condemned forever. As the last note soared from the violin of the gifted S___ts, the whole secret of art was revealed to him, and genius, eternally young, powerful, and true, crushed him with its truth. It seemed that everything which in mysterious, illusory torments had weighed upon him all his life; everything which till then had deluded and tortured him only in dreams, and from which he had fled in horror, shielding himself with deception; everything he had divined yet always feared—suddenly, at one stroke, shone before him and opened his eyes, which till that moment had stubbornly refused to distinguish between light and darkness. The truth was unbearable for eyes that looked for the first time upon what had been, what now was, and what was to be; it blinded him and seared his mind. Like lightning, it had struck instantaneously and fatally. What he had contemplated with fear and trembling his whole life had suddenly happened. All his life, it seemed, the ax had hung over his head; all his life he had been expecting, with indescribable torture, that it would fall at any moment—and it had struck at last.

He tried to escape the sentence he was under, but he had nowhere to turn; his last hope had vanished, his last pretext was gone. She who for so many years had hampered him, who would not let him live; she at whose death—as he implicitly believed—he was to have suddenly risen again, had died. He was alone at last, nothing impeded him: he was finally free! For the last time, in a paroxysm of despair, he sought to evaluate himself, to judge himself severely and inexorably, like a disinterested, impartial judge; but his impotent bow could but feebly repeat the ultimate musical phrase of a genius.... At that moment, madness, which for ten years had been lying in wait for him, struck him down.

FOUR

My convalescence was slow; but even after I had completely recovered, my mind was benumbed, and for a long time I was unable to understand just what had happened to me. There were moments when I felt I was dreaming, and I remember wishing that all that had happened to me would really turn out to have been a dream. Falling asleep at night I used to hope I would suddenly wake up in our miserable room and find Father and Mother again. . . . Eventually, however, my position became clear to me, and little by little I began to realize that I had been left alone in the world to live among strangers. And then for the first time I knew what it was to be an orphan.

I began to examine everything in those new, astonishing surroundings with intense curiosity. At first it all seemed strange and mystifying, and everything disconcerted me: the new people, the new customs, the rooms of the princely old mansion—I can see them now, large, lofty, sumptuous, but so dark and gloomy that I remember being in absolute dread of having to cross an exceedingly long reception room in which I was sure I would get lost.

I had not entirely recovered from my illness and my impressions were somber and oppressive, quite in harmony with that stately, gloomy dwelling. Moreover, there a feeling of melancholy, as yet unclear to me, that was constantly growing in my heart. I sometimes stopped in perplexity before a picture, a mirror, some intricately carved chimneypiece, or a statue that seemed to be hidden in a deep niche for the express purpose of spying on me and somehow scaring me, and having stopped there I would then forget why, what I had wanted, what I had been thinking of, and it was not until I recollected myself that I fell prey to fear and agitation and my heart beat terribly.

Of those who came to visit me from time to time while I still lay ill in bed, the one who impressed me most, except for the old doctor—was a rather elderly gentleman with an extremely serious yet kindly face, who gazed down at me with deep compassion. His face I came to love more than any of the others. I wanted so much to talk to him, but I was afraid: he always looked so despondent, spoke little and hesitantly, and was never seen to smile. This was Prince Kh___y, the man who had found me and taken me into his house.

As I began to recover, his visits gradually became less frequent. The last time he came he brought me some candy and a child's picture book, and after kissing me and making the sign of the cross over me, he bid me be more cheerful. He further consoled me by saying that soon I would have a little friend my own age, his daughter Katya, who was then in Moscow. After talking with his children's nurse, an elderly Frenchwoman, and with the maid who looked after me, he gave them instructions concerning me and departed. I did not see him again for three weeks.

The Prince lived an exceedingly solitary life in his own home. One large section of the house was occupied by the Princess, and sometimes she too did not see him for weeks on end. In the course of time I noticed that the members of the household seldom spoke of him, as though he were not living there. Everyone respected and even loved him, as was plain to see, but they regarded him as some strange and wondrous creature. He himself, it seems, was aware that he was odd and somehow not like other people, and this may have accounted for the rarity of his appearances. . . .

One morning they dressed me in immaculate fine undergarments and a black woolen dress with white weepers—which I regarded with disconsolate perplexity—then combed my hair and took me downstairs to the Princess's apartments. When they led me into her room, I stood rooted to the spot; I had never seen such opulence and splendor. But this was only a momentary impression, and a moment later I turned pale when I heard the voice of the Princess ordering them to bring me closer. Even while dressing I had felt that I was being prepared for some ordeal, though Heaven knows what had suggested such a thing to me. Altogether I had entered this new life with a peculiar mistrust of everything around me.

The princess was very gracious, however, and when she kissed me, I took courage and glanced at her. She was the same beautiful lady I had seen on first regaining consciousness. But I trembled when I kissed her hand and could not muster the strength to utter a word in reply to her questions. She told me to sit down on a low stool near her. I felt that the place had been assigned to me beforehand.

The Princess evidently wished nothing more than to become sincerely attached to me, to lavish her affection on me, and in every way to take the place of a mother. But I was incapable of understanding the opportunity that had befallen me and profited nothing from her attitude. I was given a beautiful book with pictures and told to look at it. The Princess was writing a letter and from time to time laid down her pen to talk to me, but each time I became confused and embarrassed and could say nothing sensible.

I should say that although my life had been a most unusual one—fate and various positively mysterious agents having played a large part in it—and though there had been much in it that was interesting, unaccountable, and even somewhat fantastic, I myself had turned out to be a very ordinary child, my melodramatic background notwithstanding. I was as cowed as if I had been beaten, and even a little stupid. It was the latter quality which especially displeased the Princess, and I believe she soon wearied of me—for which, it goes without saying, I had only myself to blame.

Between two and three o'clock in the afternoon, visitors had begun to arrive, and the Princess suddenly became even more affectionate and attentive to me. In reply to their questions about me, she told them that it was an extremely interesting story, and then proceeded to recount it to them in French. While she was talking, they glanced at me, shaking their heads and exclaiming. One young man trained his lorgnette on me, and an old man smelling of scent attempted to kiss me; I turned alternately crimson and pale as I sat there with downcast eyes, trembling and afraid to move. I was miserable, heartsick. I recalled the past and our garret room, thought of Father and our long, silent evenings, and of Mother—but when I thought of her my eyes filled with tears and I felt a lump in my throat. I wanted to run away, to disappear, to be alone.

Later, when the visitors had departed, the Princess's face became visibly more stern. She looked at me glumly and spoke more curtly, but I was particularly intimidated by her piercing black eyes which, with her thin lips tightly compressed, she now and then fixed on me for as long as a quarter of an hour.

In the evening I was taken back upstairs. I fell asleep in a fever and woke up during the night crying and upset because of a bad dream; but in the morning the same procedure was repeated, and I was again taken downstairs to the Princess. Eventually she herself seemed to grow weary of relating the story of my misfortunes, and her guests of commiserating over me.

Besides, I was such an ordinary child, "lacki
as I remember hearing the Princess expres
with a certain elderly lady who had aske
becoming bored with her by now?" And th
taken back upstairs, never to be taken dow

And that was the end of my being m
other hand, I was allowed to wander throug.
and to go wherever I liked. I was too painfully and proi..
miserable to be able to stay in one place for long at a time, and
was only too glad when I could at last escape from everyone in
the big rooms downstairs. I remember that I longed to talk to
the servants, but I was so afraid of annoying them that I
preferred to remain alone. My favorite pastime was to hide in a
corner, or to get behind some article of furniture where I would
be unnoticed, and then to recall and contemplate all that had
happened to me.

But the strange thing was that I seemed to have forgotten
what had happened at the very end—the whole ghastly episode
with my parents—though certain scenes flashed through my
mind which denoted the facts. Of course, I did remember
everything—the night, the violin, Father, and how I got the
money for him—but I was unable to give meaning to these
circumstances or to explain them to myself. . . . But what
weighed most heavily on my heart was the memory of those
moments when I had prayed at the side of my dead mother; just
thinking of it sent a cold chill through me, and I would utter a
faint scream and run out of my corner trembling with fear.
Every time this occurred I could scarcely breathe for the
throbbing of my heart; my whole chest ached, and I was
grief-stricken.

Yet it is not true to say that I was left alone: I was watched
closely and diligently, the Prince's orders being carried out to
the letter. He had said that I was to be given complete freedom

81

to be in any way constrained, but that they were never out of sight of me for an instant. I was aware that from time to time some member of the household or one of the servants looked into whatever room I happened to be in and disappeared without saying a word. Such vigilance was very surprising and somewhat disturbing to me. I could not understand it, and kept thinking they had an ulterior motive for taking such care of me, and that later they intended to do something to me. I remember trying to penetrate farther and farther into the house, in case I might need to know where to hide. Once I found myself on the main staircase. It was broad, carpeted, all of marble, and set out with flowers and beautiful vases. On every landing sat two tall men dressed in extraordinarily colorful clothes, with dazzling white neckcloths and gloves. I gazed at them in perplexity, unable to understand why they were sitting there in silence, doing nothing but staring at each other.

I enjoyed these solitary wanderings more and more. And there was another reason for wanting to escape from the rooms upstairs: the Prince's old aunt, who almost never went out or even left her rooms, lived up there. I have a very distinct recollection of this old woman, who was virtually the most important person in the house. Everyone observed certain formalities in his relations with her, and even the Princess, who looked so proud and imperious, was obliged to go upstairs and visit her on two fixed days of the week. These visits customarily took place in the morning and invariably began with a tedious conversation that frequently lapsed into solemn silences, during which the old lady murmured a prayer or told her rosary. The visit was always terminated by the aunt, who stood up and kissed the Princess on the lips to signify that the interview was over. Formerly the Princess had been required to visit her daily, but this duty had been mitigated at the old lady's request, and thereafter she was obliged on the other five mornings merely to send to inquire about her health.

This very old lady had lived a rather secluded life. She had never married, and on reaching the age of thirty-five had retired to a convent, where she remained for seventeen years without taking the veil. She then left the convent and went to Moscow to live with a widowed sister, the Countess L, whose health had been deteriorating year by year, and to make her peace with another sister, also a Princess Kh___a, with whom she had not been on good terms for over twenty years. But it was said that the two old ladies had been unable to live together harmoniously for a single day and had been on the point of separating a thousand times, but in the end always realized that they needed each other as a safeguard against the boredom and indispositions of old age.

Yet despite their unprepossessing way of life and the relentless boredom that reigned in their aristocratic residence in Moscow, everyone considered it his duty to continue calling on the three recluses. They were regarded as the custodians of all the aristocratic legacies and traditions, as living chronicles of the ancient boyars. Visitors from Petersburg made it a point to call on them first when they came to Moscow. Anyone who was received in their house was received anywhere.

The Countess, who had been an excellent woman, left many beautiful memories behind her when she died. After her death, the other two sisters parted. The elder, Princess Kh___a, remained in Moscow, where, like the Countess before her, she died childless. The younger, who had been in a convent, went to live with her nephew, Prince Kh___y, in Petersburg. As a compensation for her departure, the Prince's two children were left in Moscow with their grandmother, to console her and distract her in her solitude. The Princess, their mother, who was passionately fond of her children, dared not protest at being parted from them for the entire mourning period. I have forgotten to mention that at the time I came to live there, the household was in mourning; this was soon to end, however

The old Princess dressed entirely in black. She always wore a dress of some plain black material with a white starched collar gathered in fine pleats, which gave her the appearance of an almswoman. She was never without her rosary, ceremoniously attended Mass, fasted for whole days, received visits from various ecclesiastics and other sedate persons, read sacred works, and altogether led a thoroughly monastic existence. The silence upstairs was awesome; it was not possible for a door to creak without the Princess, who was as keen as a fifteen-year-old girl, sending instantly to find out the cause of the noise, though it might be no more than a squeak. Everyone spoke in whispers and walked on tiptoe, and the poor Frenchwoman, who was also quite old, was ultimately forced to give up her favorite footwear— slippers with heels. Heels were proscribed.

Two weeks after my appearance in the house, the old Princess sent to find out about me: who and what I was, how I happened to be there, and so forth. Her curiosity was promptly and respectfully satisfied. Then came a second inquiry, which was sent directly to the French governess: Why had she not yet seen me? This immediately caused a commotion; they set about combing my hair, washing my hands and face which were already quite clean teaching me the proper way to approach her, how to bow, how to address her, how to look bright and amiable, how to speak—in short, they worried me to pieces. An emissary was then dispatched from our quarter to ask whether the Princess was disposed to receive the orphan. A negative answer was returned, but a time was appointed for the following day after Mass. I was hardly able to sleep that night, but they told me later that I had been raving practically all night about visiting the Princess, and begging her to forgive me for something.

At last the hour of my presentation arrived. On entering the room, I saw a gaunt little old lady sitting in an enormous armchair. She nodded to me and put on her spectacles in order to examine me more closely. I recall that she did not like me at all. It was remarked that I was completely lacking in manners and knew neither how to curtsy nor how to kiss her hand. She launched into an interrogation which I was scarcely able to answer, and when she began to question me about my mother and father I burst into tears. The old Princess was exceedingly displeased by this display of emotion, nevertheless she undertook to comfort me and enjoined me to put my trust in God. Then she asked me when I had last been to church, and as I did not quite understand what she meant, my upbringing having been very much neglected, she was appalled. She sent for the young Princess and a consultation ensued. It was decided that I was to be taken to church the very next Sunday. The old Princess promised to pray for me in the meantime, then bid them take me away, for, as she expressed it, I had made an exceedingly painful impression on her. This was not surprising; in fact, it could hardly have been otherwise.

She quite obviously had not liked me, and the very same day sent to say that I was romping about entirely too much and could be heard all over the house, when, in fact, I had been sitting the whole day without stirring. Nevertheless, her complaint was repeated on the following day. It happened that I had just dropped a cup and broken it. The French governess and all the maids rushed in frantically, and I was moved with dispatch to a remote room, to which they all accompanied me in profound dismay.

I no longer remember how the matter ended. In any case, that was my reason for being so glad to slip away, to be alone and wander about through the spacious rooms downstairs, knowing that there, at least, I was not disturbing anyone.

I remember that I had been sitting downstairs in the reception room one day, with my head bowed and my face buried in my hands, for how many hours I do not know. I had been thinking and thinking, but my immature mind was incapable of resolving all the anguish I felt, and I grew more and more forlorn and sick at heart. All at once I heard a gentle voice speaking to me.

"What is the matter, my poor child?"

I raised my head: it was the Prince. His face expressed deep sympathy and compassion. I gazed up at him with such a crushed and woeful look that tears welled up in his large blue eyes.

"Poor little orphan!" he said, stroking my head.

"No, no, not an orphan! No!" I exclaimed, and a moan escaped me; all my feelings were aroused and I became terribly upset. I jumped up and caught hold of his hand and kissed it, covering it with my tears. "No, no, not an orphan! No!" I repeated in an imploring voice.

"My child! What is the matter with you, my poor dear Netochka? What is it?"

"Where is my mamma? Where is my mamma?" I cried, sobbing loudly, and, no longer able to conceal my distress, I fell helplessly to my knees before him. "Where is my mamma? Oh, please . . . tell me . . . where is my mamma?"

"Forgive me, my child!. . . Ah, poor little thing, I have reminded her——What have I done?. . . There, now, come with me, Netochka, come with me."

He took me by the hand and hurriedly led me out of the room. He was shaken to the depths of his being. We went into a room I had not seen before. It was the chapel. Dusk had fallen and the lights of the icon lamps flickered brightly on the gold incasements and precious stones of the holy images. The faces of the saints looked out dimly from their ornamental mountings. Everything there was entirely different from the other rooms of the house, but it was all so mysterious and somber that I was awestruck; my heart was filled with dread, and I was terribly overwrought. The Prince quickly made me kneel before the icon of the Mother of God, and he knelt beside me.

"Pray, child, pray; we will both pray!" he said in his low, hesitant voice.

But I could not pray; I was too bewildered, too full of dread. The words of my father on that last night, when I had knelt at the side of my dead mother, came back to me, and I suffered another nervous attack.

Again I fell ill and was confined to my bed, and in the course of this second illness something happened that almost resulted in my death.

One morning a familiar name seemed to ring in my ears. I had caught the name of S___ts, which one of the members of the household had mentioned at my bedside. I shuddered as recollections of the past surged up in me, and for hours lay in a veritable delirium of memories, dreams, and torments. When I awoke late that night, it was dark in the room; the night lamp had gone out, and the maid who usually stayed with me was not there. Suddenly I heard distant music. At times the sounds ceased, then grew louder, as if drawing near.

I do not know what possessed me, what resolve was suddenly born in my sick mind, but I got out of bed—how I found the strength I cannot imagine—put on my mourning dress, and groped my way along the corridor. The sound of music grew more and more distinct. Halfway down the corridor was the staircase I always used when I went down to the main rooms. The stairs were brightly lit, and people were moving about below. I shrank into a corner to avoid being seen, and as soon as it seemed possible, descended to the corridor below. The music resounded from an adjacent room. There was a hubbub of voices, as though thousands of people were assembled there. One of the doors to this room opened onto the corridor and was draped with voluminous double portières of crimson velvet. I lifted the outer one and stood between the two hangings. My heart throbbed so that I was barely able to stand on my feet. But in a few minutes, having mastered my agitation, I ventured to draw back the edge of the second hanging very slightly. To my amazement, that enormous, gloomy reception room, which I had been so afraid to enter, now blazed with thousands of lights! It was as though a sea of light had swept over me, and my eyes, accustomed to darkness, were blinded and stung with pain. A balmy gust of air like a hot wind fanned my face. Great numbers of people moved to and fro, all, it seemed, with happy, joyful faces. The women were in dazzling, resplendent attire, and everywhere I looked I saw eyes sparkling with pleasure. I stood there enthralled, feeling that I had seen all this before, perhaps in a dream. . .

Suddenly I was reminded of our garret room at twilight, the high, narrow window, the street far below in flickering lamp-light, the crimson curtains at the windows of the house opposite, the coaches crowded at the carriage porch, the stamping and snorting of spirited horses, the cries and tumult, shadowy figures in the windows, and the faint sound of distant music. . . .

So it was here, this is where that paradise had been! flashed into my mind. This is where I had wanted to go with poor Father. . . . It was not a dream after all!. . . Yes, I had seen it all before in imagination, in my dreams!. . . And fantasies kindled by my illness flared up in my mind, and I shed tears of indescribable ecstasy. . . . I looked about in search of Father. He must be here, I thought, and my heart throbbed in expectation. I could scarcely breathe.

But the music ceased, there was a hum of voices, then a whisper ran through the room. I peered eagerly at the swiftly passing faces, looking for someone. All at once there was a feeling of great excitement in the room. I caught sight of a tall, lean, elderly man standing on a dais. There was a smile on his pale face as he bent low, bowing stiffly to all sides. He held a violin in his hand. A profound silence fell over the room as though everyone were holding his breath. Every face turned expectantly toward the elderly man. He raised the violin, touched the strings with the bow, and the music began. Suddenly my heart contracted. I listened to the music with bated breath and infinite yearning: something familiar echoed in my ears; I seemed to have heard those strains before; they held a foreboding. . . a foreboding of something awesome and terrifying that was resolving itself in my heart.

The music began to swell, swifter and more piercing came the sounds. Suddenly there rang out a desperate cry, a plaintive lament, like an entreaty echoing through that crowd and dissolving in despair. It became more and more familiar and spoke to my heart, but my heart refused to believe it. I clenched my teeth to keep from moaning with anguish, clung to the curtains to keep from falling. . . . Now and then I shut my eyes and suddenly opened them again, thinking it was a dream, that I would wake up to some terrible, familiar moment, and I seemed to see that last night, to hear the very same sounds. And opening my eyes I peered eagerly at the crowd, wanting to convince myself. . . . No, they were not the same people, those were not the same faces. . . .

It seemed to me that everyone there was waiting expectantly as I was, and suffering with me; that they all wanted to utter the same terrible moans and cries, and, though they remained silent and were not tormenting their souls, the moans and cries mounted nonetheless, growing ever more plaintive, prolonged, and distraught. Suddenly the last, long, terrible cry rang out and

I was transfixed . . . There was no longer any doubt—it was the same, the very same cry! I recognized it; I had heard it before; and as on that other night, it pierced my soul.

"Father! Father!" flashed through my mind. "He is here—it is he—he is calling me!. . . That is his violin!"

A roar of applause, like a moan escaping from the crowd, shook the whole room. A desperate cry was torn from my breast. I could no longer bear it. I flung back the portières and rushed into the room.

"Papa! Papa! It's you! Where are you?" I cried, almost frantic.

I do not know how I managed to reach the tall old man: the crowd fell back to let me pass. I flung myself on him with an anguished cry; I thought I was embracing Father. . . .

All at once I saw that I was held by large, bony hands that lifted me into the air. Black eyes were riveted on me as if they would consume me in their fire. I looked at the old man. "No, this is not Father—this is his murderer!" flashed through my mind. I was seized with a kind of frenzy, and suddenly it seemed to me that I heard his laughter ringing out above me, and that laughter reverberated through the room in one concerted cry. I lost consciousness.

FIVE

That was my second and last period of illness.

When I opened my eyes again, I saw leaning over me the face of a child, a little girl my own age, and my first gesture was to extend my hand to her. From the moment I saw her, my whole soul was pervaded with happiness as with some sweet promise. Imagine an utterly winsome little face of a striking, scintillating beauty, one of those faces before which one stops as if transfixed, confused and quivering with delight; one that makes us grateful she exists, that our glance has fallen upon her, that she has chanced to pass our way. This was the Prince's daughter Katya, who had just returned from Moscow. She smiled at my gesture, and my weakened nerves began to ache with a sweet ecstasy.

The little Princess called her father, who stood nearby talking to the doctor.

"Well, thank God! Thank God!" said the Prince, taking my hand, and his face beamed with genuine feeling. "I am so glad, so very glad!" he went on, speaking with characteristic rapidity. "And this is Katya, my daughter. Now you will have a friend. Get well soon, Netochka. . . . What a naughty girl—she gave me such a fright!"

I made a rapid recovery, and within a few days was up and about. Katya came to my bedside every morning, always smiling, always bubbling with laughter. I looked forward to her coming as to some great happiness; I was longing to kiss her! But the frolicsome little girl remained with me only a few minutes at a time. It was impossible for her to sit still; to be constantly in motion, to run and skip and raise a racket and commotion all through the house was an absolute necessity for her. She announced to me from the first that she would not come often because she found it dreadfully dull sitting with me, but that she felt so sorry for me she could not help coming, and when I had recovered it would be better.

Her first words every morning were: "Well, have you recovered?"

But as I was still thin and pale and only a wan smile appeared on my doleful face, the Princess always frowned, shook her head, and stamped her little foot in vexation.

"Didn't I tell you yesterday to get better? They're probably not giving you enough to eat, are they?

"No, not very much . . ." I answered timidly, for I was already afraid of her.

I was so terribly eager for her to like me that I had misgivings about my every word and gesture. I became more and more enraptured with her every time she appeared. I could not take my eyes off her when she was with me, and when she had gone I continued to gaze enthralled at the spot where she had stood. I began to dream about her. And when she was not there I invented long conversations with her: I was her friend; we frolicked and played pranks together, and when reprimanded for something we had done wept together—in short, I dreamed of her as if I were in love. I was desperately anxious to recover and grow plump, as she advised me, just as soon as possible.

Sometimes when Katya came running into my room in the morning, instantly calling out: "Not well yet? Still so thin?" I quailed as if I were guilty of something. But to her, nothing could have been more positively astounding than my inability to recover overnight, and she began to be genuinely cross about it.

"Well, how would you like to have me bring you some cake today?" she said to me one day. "You eat that and you'll soon get plump."

"Yes, do bring some," I said, delighted at the prospect of seeing her again.

When she came to inquire about my health, Katya generally sat down in a chair facing me and began at once to scrutinize me with her black eyes. At first, when she was getting acquainted with me, she kept examining me from head to foot in the most naive astonishment. But conversation flagged. Though I longed to talk to her, I was always timid in her presence and frequently taken aback by her abrupt sallies.

"Why so quiet?" she began after one of our silences.

"What is your Papa doing?" I inquired, delighted that there was one phrase with which I could always start a conversation.

"Nothing. Papa's all right. Today I drank two cups of coffee instead of one. How many did you drink?"

"One."

Another silence.

"Falstaff tried to bite me today."

"Is that a dog?"

"Yes, it is. Haven't you ever seen him?"

"Yes, I've seen him."

"Then why did you ask?"

And since I did not know what to answer the Princess again looked at me in surprise.

"Tell me, do you enjoy having me come and talk to you?"

"Yes, I do, very much. Come often."

"That's what they told me—that you would enjoy it if I came to see you—but do get well soon. I'm going to bring you some cake today. . . . But why don't you ever talk?"

"Just because . . ."

"You're always thinking, I suppose."

"Yes, I think a lot."

"They tell me I talk a lot but don't think much. Do you think it's bad to talk?"

"No, I'm happy when you talk."

"Hm-m . . I'll ask Madame Leotard, she knows everything. But what do you think about?"

"I think about you," I replied, after a pause.

"Do you enjoy that?"

"Yes."

"Does that mean you love me?"

"Yes."

"Well, I don't love you yet. You're too thin! Listen, I'm going to bring you that cake. Well, good-bye!"

And kissing me almost in flight the Princess vanished from the room.

But after dinner she appeared with the cake. She ran in, laughing hilariously and in high glee, because she was bringing me something that had been forbidden me.

"Eat some more, eat a lot—it's my cake, I didn't eat any. Well, good-bye!" And she was gone in a flash.

Another time she suddenly flew into my room at an unaccustomed hour, her black curls in wild disorder, her eyes sparkling and her cheeks flaming, all of which showed that she had been running and skipping about the house for an hour or two.

"Do you know how to play battledore and shuttlecock?" she cried, breathless and speaking rapidly in her haste to be off again.

"No," I answered, acutely regretting that I could not say yes.

"What a funny girl! Get well, then, and I'll teach you. I only came to find out. I'm playing with Madame Leotard. Good-bye, they're waiting for me."

At last I was up and about, though still weak and enervated. My first thought was of no longer being separated from Katya. I felt irresistibly drawn to her and could not see enough of her, which was surprising to Katya. The attraction to her was so strong, and I surrendered to this new feeling with such ardor, that she could not help noticing it, and in the beginning it struck her as being extraordinarily odd. I remember once, when we were playing some game, that I could not restrain myself, and throwing my arms around her neck began kissing her. She freed herself from my embrace, took hold of my hands, and frowning as if I had offended her in some way said:

"What's the matter with you? What are you kissing me for?"

I was as disconcerted as if I had done something wrong, and so startled by the abruptness of her question that I could not utter a word in reply. The Princess drew up her shoulders to express her hopeless perplexity (one of her characteristic gestures), and, abandoning the game, sat down in a corner of the sofa and contemplated me for a long time, as though she were working out some new problem that had unexpectedly arisen in her mind. This too was characteristic of her whenever she was in a quandary. For my part, it took me a long time to get used to these sharp and unexpected revelations of her character.

In the beginning I blamed myself, thinking that there really were a great many things about me that were strange. And although this was true, I was nonetheless tortured by doubts: why could I not have become Katya's friend from the first and have been liked by her once and for all? This failure on my part grieved me sorely, and I was ready to cry at every sharp word and dubious look from her. And since everything that concerned Katya moved very swiftly, my sorrow increased by leaps and bounds.

Within a few days I noticed that she had taken a dislike to me, and had even begun to feel a repugnance for me. Everything was done hastily and vehemently by this little girl—one might have said harshly had there not been in the lightning-quick impulses of her straightforward, naively frank nature a true and noble grace. It had begun by her feeling first doubt, then a certain contempt for me, which originated, I believe, in my being absolutely incapable of playing any sort of game. The Princess liked romping and frolicking about, was lively, nimble, and strong, while I was the exact opposite. I was still weak from my illness, was quiet, pensive, and did not enjoy playing; in fact, I was entirely wanting in the faculties that appealed to Katya. And, on top of this, I could not bear to feel that I was displeasing to anyone. I at once became so melancholy and disconsolate that I lacked strength to make amends for my mistake and to improve the poor impression I had made—in other words, I became completely crushed. Katya was in no way able to understand this.

At first she really intimidated me when, after having gone to the trouble to teach me how to play battledore and shuttlecock —sometimes for an hour at a time to no avail—she would gaze at me in astonishment (another habit of hers). And then when I became so unhappy that I was on the verge of tears, she would think about me for a moment or two without understanding either me or her own reflections, and then leave me to go off and play by herself without asking me to join her again or even speaking to me for days. I was dumbfounded by such behavior and could not endure her disdain. This new loneliness became almost as painful to me as my former solitude; again I grew pensive and melancholy, and somber thoughts preyed on my mind.

Madame Leotard, who looked after us, had become aware of the change in our relations, and when she noticed my enforced solitude went straight to the little Princess and chided her for not being able to get along with me. The Princess knit her brows, drew up her shoulders, and declared that there was nothing she could do with me, that I did not know how to play and was always thinking about something, but when her brother Sasha returned from Moscow, it would be far more fun.

Madame Leotard was not satisfied with this answer, however, and rebuked her for leaving me alone while I was still sick. She explained to her that I could not be as playful and high-spirited as she was, which was a good thing in any case, she added, as Katya was much too exuberant. She went on to tell her that she had been guilty of one thing and another, had almost been bitten by the bulldog a few days earlier, and, in fact, scolded her unmercifully. It ended in her sending Katya to make peace with me at once.

Katya listened to Madame Leotard very attentively, as if she had actually begun understanding something for the first time and saw the justice of her reasoning. She left her hoop, which she had been rolling up and down the room, and with a very serious mien came to me and said:

"Would you like to play?"

"No," I replied, always apprehensive for both myself and Katya when Madame Leotard scolded her.

"Then what would you like to do?"

"I'll just sit here; it's hard for me to run; only don't be angry with me, Katya, because I love you very much."

"Well, then, I'm going to play by myself," said Katya quietly and deliberately, as if to her surprise it had turned out that she was not to blame after all. "Good-bye, I won't be angry with you."

"Good-bye," I said, getting up and giving her my hand.

"Perhaps you'd like us to kiss?" she said, after having thought a moment; she had no doubt recalled our recent scene and was trying to be as nice to me as possible in order to be done with me quickly and amicably.

"If you like," I replied with a diffident hope.

She came up to me, serious and unsmiling, and kissed me. Having thus acquitted herself of her obligation, having done even more than was required of her to appease the poor girl to whom she had been sent to make peace, she ran off, satisfied and gay, and before long her laughter and shouting echoed through the house until, exhausted and breathless, she flung herself down on a sofa to rest and gather fresh energy. All that evening she kept looking at me suspiciously; I probably seemed very strange to her. It was obvious that she wanted to talk to me about something, to clear up some perplexity that had arisen in her mind concerning me, but on that occasion, for what reason I do not know, she restrained herself.

The mornings generally began with Katya's lessons. Madame Leotard was teaching her French, and her instruction consisted of going over the grammar in selections from La Fontaine. Katya was not taught very much, for it was all they could do to get her to sit still for two hours a day with her books. She had reluctantly consented to this arrangement at her father's request and her mother's insistence, but once she had given her word, conscientiously abided by the agreement. She had the rare ability of quick and ready comprehension. But even in this she had her little idiosyncrasies: if there was something she did not understand, she immediately set about thinking it out for herself, as she could not endure explanations, which for some reason were humiliating to her. It was said that there were times when she spent whole days struggling with a problem she was unable to solve, and became angry when she could not master it without someone's help. Only after completely exhausting herself, and then as a last resort, would she go to Madame Leotard and ask her help with some problem she had not succeeded in solving herself. It was the same with everything she did. Though it was not immediately apparent, she thought a great deal. At the same time, she was naive for her age; sometimes she would ask questions that were positively silly, while at other times her responses revealed the most penetrating insight and subtlety.

When I was at last able to study, Madame Leotard tested me to see how much I knew, and finding that I read very well but wrote very poorly, considered it absolutely imperative to start teaching me French.

I made no objection, and one morning found myself sitting at the schoolroom table with Katya. As luck would have it, Katya was exceedingly dull-witted and bemused that day, so much so that Madame Leotard was incredulous. I, on the other hand, eager to please Madame Leotard with my diligence, had learned the whole French alphabet before the lesson was over. By the end of the lesson she had become quite cross with Katya.

"Look at her," she said, pointing to me, "a sick child, yet in her first lesson she has learned ten times more than you have. Aren't you ashamed?"

"She knows more than I do?" Katya asked in consternation, "But she just learned the French alphabet!"

"And how many lessons did it take you to learn it?"

"Three."

"She has learned it in one. That means she learns three times faster than you and will outstrip you in no time. Isn't that so?"

Katya considered this for a moment and suddenly her face turned red as fire, proving the justice of Madame Leotard's rebuke. To turn red, to burn with shame, was Katya's first reaction to any sort of failure, disappointment, wounded pride, or to being caught in some prank—to almost anything, in fact. On this occasion, she had to force back her tears, but she said nothing and merely looked at me as if she would have liked to consume me with her gaze. I surmised at once what was wrong. The poor girl was proud and full of self-conceit. When we left

Madame Leotard, I wanted to dissipate her vexation as quickly as possible by persuading her that I was not to blame for what the Frenchwoman had said to her, but Katya remained silent, as if not hearing me.

An hour later, she came into the room where I was sitting with a book, still thinking about her, dumbfounded and dismayed that again she would not speak to me. Glancing at me petulantly, she sat down as usual on the sofa, and for the next half hour kept her gaze fixed on me. Finally I could bear it no longer and glanced at her questioningly.

"Do you know how to dance?" she asked.

"No, I don't."

"Well, I do."

Silence.

"And can you play the piano?"

"No, I can't do that either."

"Well, I can. And that's very hard to learn."

I made no response.

"Madame Leotard says you're cleverer than I am."

"Madame Leotard was angry with you," I said.

"Do you think Papa will be angry too?"

"I don't know," I replied.

Again a silence; the Princess tapped her little foot impatiently.

"And are you going to make fun of me now, just because you're smarter than I am?" she said at last, no longer able to bear her chagrin.

"Oh, no, no!" I cried, jumping up and throwing my arms around her.

Suddenly we heard the voice of Madame Leotard, who had been observing us and listening to our conversation for the last five minutes.

"Aren't you ashamed to ask such a question, or even to think such a thing? For shame!" she continued "You've grown envious of the poor child, and so you boast of being able to dance and play the piano. Disgraceful! I shall inform the Prince of all this."

The Princess's cheeks glowed like a sunset.

"That's a wicked feeling. You have offended her with your questions. Her parents were poor and could not engage teachers for her; she studied by herself, because she's a good girl. And she has a kind heart; you ought to love her, but instead you want to quarrel with her. For shame! For shame! And here she is, an orphan. She has no one. You'll be boasting next of being a Princess when she is not. I shall leave you alone now. Think about what I have said to you, and mend your ways."

The Princess thought about it for exactly two days. For two days her laughter and shouting were not heard. Waking at night I could hear her arguing with Madame Leotard in her sleep. She even grew somewhat thinner in the course of those two days, and her naturally high color glowed less vividly in her bright little face. At last, on the third day, we happened to meet in one of the big rooms downstairs. The Princess was leaving her mother's apartments, but on seeing me sat down opposite me and quite near. I waited in fear and trembling for what might happen.

"Netochka, why did I have to be scolded on account of you?" she finally asked.

"It was not on account of me, Katenka," I replied, hastily vindicating myself.

"But Madame Leotard says I offended you."

"No, Katenka, no—you haven't offended me."

The Princess drew up her shoulders as a sign of perplexity.

"Then why are you always crying?" she asked after a brief pause.

"I won't cry if you don't want me to," I answered tearfully.

She again shrugged her shoulders. "Did you always cry before?"

I made no reply.

"Why are you living with us?" she suddenly asked after a pause.

I looked at her in surprise and felt as if something had pierced my heart. "Because I'm an orphan," I said, having mustered my courage.

"Did you have a papa and mamma?"

"Yes."

"Well, didn't they love you?"

"Yes . . . they loved me," I said, hardly able to speak.

"Were they poor?"

"Yes."

"Very poor?"

"Yes."

"Didn't they teach you anything?"

"They taught me to read."

"Did you have any toys?"

"No."

"Did you have cake?"

"No."

"How many rooms did you have?"

"One."

"But were there servants?"

"No, there were no servants."

"Then who did the work?"

"I used to run the errands myself."

The Princess's questions wounded me more and more. My memories, my loneliness, and her incredulity all combined to shock and hurt me. I was quivering with agitation, choked with tears.

"You must be glad to be living with us."

I was silent.

"Did you have a pretty dress?"

"No."

"Was it ugly?"

"Yes."

"I saw your dress—they showed it to me."

"Why are you asking me these things?" I said, springing up from my chair and trembling with an emotion I had never known before. "Why are you questioning me?" I went on, flushing with indignation. "Why are you making fun of me?"

The Princess flared up, but instantly controlled her emotion. "I'm not making fun of you," she said. "I only wanted to find out whether it was true that your papa and mamma were poor."

"Why do you ask me about my papa and mamma?" I cried, bursting into tears of heartfelt anguish. "Why do you question me like this about them? What did they ever do to you, Katya?"

Katya was confused and did not know what to say. Just then the Prince came in.

"What's the matter, Netochka?" he asked, seeing me in tears. "What's the matter?" he repeated, after glancing at Katya, whose face was flaming. "What have you been talking about? Why have you been quarreling? . . . Netochka, what have you quarreled about?"

Unable to answer, I grasped the Prince's hand and kissed it, covering it with my tears.

"Katya, don't lie to me! What has been going on here?"

But Katya was incapable of lying.

"I told her I had seen what an ugly dress she wore when she still lived with her papa and mamma."

"Who showed it to you? Who dared to show it to you?"

"I saw it by myself," retorted Katya resolutely.

"Very well then! I know you, and I am sure you will never tell this to anyone. And what else?"

"She started to cry and asked me why I was making fun of her papa and mamma."

"Then you were making fun of them?"

Although she had not actually made fun of them, it was obviously Katya's intention, as I had realized from the first. She made no reply, which meant that she admitted to the offense.

"Go to her at once and ask her forgiveness," said the Prince, pointing to me.

The Princess, white as a sheet, did not move.

"Well?" said the Prince.

"I don't want to!" Katya at last murmured under her breath, but with a very determined look.

"Katya!"

"No! I don't want to! I don't want to!" she suddenly cried stamping her foot, and her eyes flashed. "I don't want to ask her forgiveness, Papa. I don't like her. I won't live with her any longer. It's not my fault that she cries all day. I don't want to, I don't want to!"

"Come with me," said the Prince, taking her hand and leading her off to his study. "Go upstairs, Netochka."

I wanted to rush to the Prince and intercede for Katya, but he sternly repeated his order and I went upstairs, deathly cold with fear. When I reached our room, I dropped onto the sofa and buried my head in my hands. I counted the minutes as I waited impatiently for Katya to return, feeling that I wanted to throw myself at her feet. Finally she returned, and, walking past me without a word, sat down in a corner. Her eyes were red and her cheeks puffy from weeping. All my resolution vanished. I looked at her in fear, and my fear made it impossible for me to move from where I sat.

I blamed myself with all my heart and sincerely tried to persuade myself that it had all been my fault. A thousand times I wanted to go to Katya, and a thousand times hesitated, not knowing how she would behave toward me. The whole day passed in this way, and the next one too. But on the third day toward evening Katya brightened up and started rolling her hoop through the rooms; she soon abandoned this diversion, however, and sat alone in a corner. Just before bedtime she suddenly turned toward me, took a step or two in my direction, and having opened her mouth to say something stopped, turned around, and went off to bed.

After the second day Madame Leotard began to wonder about Katya and to question her as to why she was so quiet, and whether she felt ill. Katya made some reply and was about to take up her shuttlecock, but had no sooner turned away from Madame Leotard than her face flushed and she began to cry. She ran out of the room to prevent my seeing her.

But finally it was all settled: exactly three days after our quarrel, she suddenly appeared in my room, and, approaching me with a certain diffidence said:

"Papa says I must ask your forgiveness. Will you forgive me?"

I threw my arms around her, breathless with excitement.

"Yes! Yes!" I said.

"Papa says we should kiss each other. Will you kiss me?"

In answer I began kissing her hands, covering them with my tears. When I looked at Katya, I saw something I had never seen before. Her lips moved tremulously, her chin quivered, and her eyes were moist, but she quickly overcame her agitation and broke into a smile.

"I'll go and tell Papa that I've kissed you and asked your forgiveness," she said softly and reflectively. "I haven't seen him for three days; he forbade me even to come to his room till I had done this," she added, after a pause.

After she had said this, she thoughtfully and hesitantly went downstairs, as though uncertain of how her father would receive her.

An hour later, there was an outburst of shouting and laughter upstairs, followed by the barking of Falstaff, the clatter of something being overturned and broken, and of books flying to the floor. And when I again heard the hoop humming and bouncing through the rooms I knew that Katya was reconciled to her father, and my heart throbbed with joy.

But she did not come near me and was evidently trying to avoid talking to me, instead of which I had the signal honor of having aroused her curiosity. She sat down opposite me where she could observe me more closely. Her scrutiny became increasingly ingenuous; in short, this pampered, self-willed girl, whom everyone in the house indulged and cherished, could not understand how on more than one occasion she had happened to find me in her way when she had absolutely no desire to see me. Hers was a fine, good little heart, however, which always led her to find the right path simply by instinct.

Her father, whom she adored, had the greatest influence on her. Her mother loved her to distraction, but was terribly strict with her; Katya had inherited her willfulness, pride, and strength of character, but had also adopted all her whims, which amounted to a form of moral tyranny. The Princess had a rather odd conception of raising a child, and Katya's upbringing was a strange combination of pampering, leniency, and relentless severity. What was permitted one day was suddenly and without apparent reason forbidden the next, which outraged the child's sense of justice. . . . But that story comes later.

I shall mention only that she was already capable of making a distinction in her relations with her mother and father. With the latter she was herself, completely open, guileless, and frank. With her mother she was just the opposite—reticent, mistrustful, yet implicitly obedient. Her obedience was given out of neither conviction nor sincerity, however, but simply because it was in the prescribed order of things. I will explain this later. . . . But to give Katya her due, I will say that she understood her mother, and in submitting to her was fully cognizant of her boundless love. That this love was at times morbidly excessive was a circumstance of which the young Princess took liberal advantage. Alas, it was an advantage that was to prove of scant benefit to the hotheaded little girl.

I was hardly able to understand what was happening to me. Everything in me was agitated by a new and inexplicable emotion, and it is no exaggeration to say that I suffered agonies from this new feeling. To be brief—and may I be forgiven for what I now say—I was in love with my Katya. Yes, it was love, real love, love with all its tears and joys, passionate love. What had attracted me to her? What had engendered such love? It had begun with my first glimpse of her, when all my emotions were sweetly stirred at the sight of a child who was as lovely as an angel. Everything about her was beautiful; not one of her flaws was inborn, all had been implanted in her and subsequently manifested themselves in conditions of conflict. The original beauty, which with the passage of time had assumed a false form, was apparent, and everything about her, beginning with this conflict, radiated confidence and presaged a splendid future.

Not I alone, but everyone loved and admired her. When we were taken out for our afternoon walk, passers-by used to stop in astonishment at the sight of her, and it was not unusual to hear exclamations of wonder follow in the wake of this happy child. She was born for happiness, she must have been born for happiness, that being the first impression she made on everyone. Perhaps what had stirred me in the beginning had been an aesthetic feeling, an artistic awareness which her beauty had awakened in me for the first time—and therein lay the cause of my love.

The Princess's chief flaw, or, rather, the chief element in her character that strove irrepressibly for embodiment in outward form—but which was naturally in abeyance when she found herself in a state of conflict—was pride. This pride extended even to the merest trifles and verged on such self-conceit that if, for instance, she met with any contradiction whatsoever, she was not offended or angered by it, but simply incredulous. She could not conceive of the possibility of something's being other than what she wished it to be. Nevertheless, her sense of justice always gained the upper hand. When convinced that she was wrong, she conceded the point with alacrity and no more was heard of it. And if her attitude toward me had changed during that period, I can only explain it as the consequence of a deep antipathy which had troubled the harmony of her being. It must have been that; she always entered into her enthusiasms too passionately, and she was ultimately led to the right path only by example or experience. Though the results of all she undertook were beautiful and true, they were obtained at the cost of continual deviations and errors.

Katya very soon had enough of observing me and at last decided to leave me in peace. She behaved as if I were not even living in the house and refused to address a superfluous word to me, in fact, hardly said what was necessary. I was excluded from all her games, but it was done so adroitly that it almost seemed to have been at my wish. Our lessons followed their usual course, and if I was held up to her as an example of aptitude and sobriety, I no longer had the honor of wounding her pride, which was so uncommonly susceptible that it could be wounded even by our bulldog, Sir John Falstaff.

Falstaff, a cold-blooded, phlegmatic dog, could be fierce as a tiger when teased, fierce to the point of defying his master's authority. Another of his characteristics was that he had absolutely no love for anyone, but his natural and most powerful enemy was unquestionably the old Princess. . . . However, that story will come later.

The egotistical little Princess tried by every means to overcome Falstaff's truculency: she could not bear to feel that there was a single creature in the house who did not acknowledge her authority and power, who did not defer to her and love her. And so she decided to attack Falstaff herself. Since she wanted to dominate everyone, to wield power, how could Falstaff possibly escape his fate? Nevertheless, the recalcitrant bulldog refused to yield to her.

One day we were both sitting in the large reception room downstairs when the bulldog lethargically settled down in the middle of the room to enjoy his afterdinner nap. And it was at that very moment that the Princess took it into her head to conquer him and bend him to her will. She abandoned her game then and there and cautiously approached him on tiptoe, beckoning to him with coaxing gestures and calling him by the most affectionate pet names. But even before she could get near him he bared his terrible fangs, and the Princess paused. Her intention had been only to go up to him and stroke him (a privilege he allowed absolutely no one but his favorite, Katya's mother) and afterward to induce him to follow her—a difficult feat and one that entailed a serious risk, as Falstaff would not hesitate to snap at her hand or to tear her to pieces if he considered it necessary. He was as strong as a bear, and from a distance I watched Katya's stratagems with anxiety and dread. But it was not easy to dissuade her all at once, and even the sight of Falstaff's teeth, which he had bared most uncivilly, was not enough to deter her.

When she saw that it was impossible to approach him directly, the Princess was in a quandary and began circling her enemy. Falstaff did not stir. She made a second attempt, this time diminishing the diameter of the circle significantly. Then she made a third circle, but when she reached the point which to Falstaff was evidently an inviolable boundary, he again bared his teeth. The Princess stamped her foot, walked off and sat down on the sofa, vexed and irresolute.

Ten minutes later, having thought of a way to lure him, she left the room and returned with a supply of little cakes and biscuits. She had decided to change her tactics. But Falstaff was unmoved, probably because he had already eaten his fill. He did not so much as glance at the bit of biscuit she threw to him; however, when the Princess again advanced to the boundary of what Falstaff evidently considered his territory, she met with more salient opposition. Falstaff raised his head, bared his teeth, and with a low growl made as if to get up. The Princess flushed angrily, and flinging down the cakes returned to the sofa and sat down.

She was decidedly perturbed. Her cheeks glowed, her little foot tapped the carpeted floor, and her eyes brimmed with tears of exasperation. And when her gaze happened to fall on me, all the blood rushed to her head. She sprang up, and with a very determined step walked straight up to the terrifying dog.

This time Falstaff must have been taken by surprise. He let his enemy cross the border, and not until she was but a step or two from him did he greet the imprudent girl with a vicious snarl. Katya was stopped, but only momentarily, then continued her advance undaunted. I was numb with fear. I had never seen her so exhilarated; her eyes shone with victory triumphant. She would have made a wonderful picture. Unflinching before the menacing glare of the infuriated bulldog she stood her ground. A terrifying growl issued from his bristly chest; in another moment he would have torn her to pieces. But with a proud gesture the Princess put her little hand on his back and gave it three triumphant strokes. For an instant the bulldog seemed uncertain. That was the most dreadful moment; then he ponderously got to his feet, stretched himself, and, having no doubt decided that it was not worthwhile to have dealings with children, impassively walked out of the room. The Princess, exultant, took her stand on the conquered territory and darted an enigmatic look at me, a gratified, intoxicated look of victory. She saw that I was white as a sheet and smiled. But all at once her cheeks took on a deathly pallor. She was hardly able to reach the sofa, where she sank down almost in a faint.

My infatuation with Katya was boundless. From that day, when I had experienced such great fear for her, I was no longer able to control myself. I was pining away with love for her; a thousand times I was ready to throw myself on her neck, but fear held me rooted to the spot. I remember trying to avoid her lest she see my agitation, but once, when she unexpectedly entered the room where I had been hiding, I started, and my heart throbbed so that I felt dizzy. I believe that my little minx noticed it and for a day or two was herself in a state of confusion. However, she soon accepted this too as being in the natural order of things.

Thus a whole month passed during which I continued to suffer in silence. My feelings had undergone an indescribable strain, if one may so express it. I am by nature infinitely long-suffering, and an outburst or any sudden manifestation of emotion occurs only in a crisis. It must be realized that during all this time Katya and I had exchanged no more than half a dozen words; but from certain elusive signs, I had gradually begun to perceive that all this had come about not through her disregard or indifference to me, but from a deliberate evasiveness, almost as though she had promised herself to keep me within certain bounds. But by then I could no longer sleep at night, and during the day was unable to conceal my confusion from Madame Leotard. My love for Katya even led me to do strange things. Once I stole one of her handkerchiefs, and another time a little ribbon that she wound in her hair, and I would kiss them all night long and shed tears over them.

In the beginning I had been tortured, mortified by Katya's indifference, but by this time I was in a state of such inner turmoil that I no longer knew what I was feeling. Thus new impressions were crowding out the old, and in this new life memories of my melancholy past were gradually being replaced and losing their power to cause me pain.

I remember sometimes waking up at night, getting up, and approaching Katya's bed on tiptoe. In the dim light of our night lamp, I would stand and gaze at the sleeping Princess by the hour. Often I sat on the bed beside her, and bending down felt her hot breath on my face. Gently, trembling with fear, I kissed her hands, her hair, her shoulders, and her little foot if it happened to peep out from under the blanket. Gradually I began to notice—for I had not let her out of my sight for a whole month—that Katya was growing more pensive day by day. She was beginning to lose her sanguine disposition: sometimes not a sound was heard from her the whole day, at other times she raised an unprecedented uproar. She became irritable, exacting, often blushed and lost her temper, and even went so far as to indulge in petty acts of cruelty toward me. All at once she would be unwilling to sit next to me at dinner, as though she felt repelled by me; or she would unexpectedly go off to her mother and stay there the whole day, knowing that I was desperately longing for her; or she would decide to sit and stare at me by the hour, till I was so excruciatingly embarrassed I did not know what to do and sat there, blushing and turning pale by turns yet not daring to get up and leave the room.

On two occasions Katya complained of feeling feverish, though she had never been known to suffer from any sort of illness before. Then suddenly one morning, special arrangements were afoot: at the little Princess's express wish, she was being moved downstairs to be with her mother, who had almost died of fright when Katya had complained of not feeling well.

It must be remarked that Katya's mother was exceedingly displeased with me and with every aspect of the change in her daughter, which she had noticed and ascribed to me and to the influence of my sullen nature, as she expressed it, on her daughter's character. She would have separated us long before but had postponed it thus far knowing that she would have to face a serious argument with the Prince, who as a rule yielded to her in everything but at times became adamant and uncompromising. She did not entirely understand the Prince.

I was shocked by the Princess's move and spent a whole week in a state of the most agonizing tension, tormented by longing and racking my brains over the reason for Katya's antipathy to me. My soul was lacerated by sorrow, and a sense of righteous indignation rose up in my wounded heart. Suddenly a feeling of pride was born in me, and when Katya and I met at the hour we were always taken out for a walk, I looked at her with such gravity and independence, and was so unlike my former self, that she was quite astonished.

These changes occurred in me only sporadically, of course, and afterward my heart ached even more poignantly, and I grew weaker and more fainthearted than ever.

Finally, one morning, to my great bewilderment and joy, the little Princess came back upstairs. The first thing she did was to fling herself on Madame Leotard's neck with a wild shout of laughter and announce that she had returned to us; then, after nodding to me, she begged to be released from lessons that day and proceeded to spend the whole morning frolicking and scampering about. I had never seen her so vivacious and gay. But toward evening she quieted down and grew pensive, and again a look of sadness clouded her little face. When her mother came to see her in the evening I could see that Katya was making an unnatural effort to appear cheerful. But no sooner had her mother gone than she dissolved in tears. I was dumbfounded. Katya noticed my concern and left the room.

Apparently something unforeseen, a crisis of some sort, was brewing in her. Her mother consulted doctors and sent for Madame Leotard daily to question her in minute detail about her daughter, and orders were given to watch her constantly. I alone sensed the truth, and my heart throbbed with hope.

In a word, the little romance was drawing toward its consummation. The third day after Katya had come back upstairs, I noticed that she kept casting long and wonderfully loving looks at me all morning. Several times I met her gaze, and each time we both blushed and cast down our eyes as though ashamed. At last the Princess broke into a laugh and went out of the room.

When the clock struck three, we set about getting ready for our walk. All at once Katya came up to me.

"Your shoe is untied," she said. "Let me tie it for you."

I started to bend down and tie it myself, blushing red as a cherry because Katya had at last spoken to me.

"Let me!" she said impatiently, having begun to laugh.

She bent down, and taking firm hold of my foot placed it on her knee and tied my shoe. I could hardly breathe, such sweet dismay left me helpless. When the shoe was tied, she stood up and surveyed me from head to foot.

"Your throat is not covered," she said, lightly touching my bare neck with her little finger. "Here, I'll tie it over for you."

I made no protest. She untied my kerchief and retied it in her own way.

"Otherwise you might get a cough," she said with a mischievous smile, her melting black eyes twinkling at me.

I was beside myself; I knew neither what was happening to me nor what had come over Katya. But, God be praised, our walk was soon over; had it lasted much longer I could not have restrained myself and would have flung myself on her and kissed her there in the street. As we went upstairs, I succeeded in slyly kissing her on the shoulder. She quivered, but did not say anything.

In the evening she was dressed up and taken downstairs where the Princess was entertaining guests. But that night there was a dreadful turmoil in the house. Katya had suffered some sort of nervous attack and the Princess was frightened to death. The doctor came, but he did not know what to say. Everything was ascribed to childhood diseases, of course, and to Katya's age, but I thought differently. In the morning she came back upstairs looking rosy, merry, and as inexhaustibly healthy as ever, but full of whims and fancies that were quite unlike her.

In the first place, she refused the entire morning to obey Madame Leotard. Then she took it into her head to visit the old Princess. The old lady could not endure her little grandniece, had always been antagonistic to her and never wanted to see her, but on this occasion, for some reason, she decided to receive her. The visit began very amicably, and for the first hour they got on well together. The little rogue had decided to beg forgiveness for all her past misdeeds, her romping and shouting and never giving the Princess any peace. The old Princess, with tears in her eyes, solemnly forgave her. But then the little imp decided to go even further. She conceived the notion of recounting certain pranks which thus far were no more than schemes, projects for the future, and then meekly and piously pretending to have repented of them. The narrow-minded old lady was in raptures: her prospective victory over Katya—the pet and idol of the whole household, who could even make her mother gratify her whims—flattered her vanity.

And so the little minx proceeded to confess that she had planned to glue a visiting card to the Princess's dress, hide Falstaff under her bed, break her spectacles, carry off all her books and replace them with her mother's French novels, get hold of some firecrackers and scatter them over the floor, hide a pack of cards in her pocket, and on and on, one prank worse than another. The old lady was beside herself and turned livid with rage. Finally Katya could not control her hilarious laughter and fled from the room.

The old Princess lost no time in sending for Katya's mother. And there began a whole procedure, with the Princess spending two hours tearfully pleading with the aunt to forgive Katya and not to insist on her being punished, in view of the fact that she was ill. At first the old lady refused to listen to her and announced that she was leaving the house the next day. She was mollified only after the Princess had given her word that she would appease the old Princess's righteous indignation by punishing her daughter as soon as she was well.

Katya was severely reprimanded and taken downstairs to her mother's apartments. But the little minx managed to escape after dinner. I had stolen downstairs and found her about to come up. She had opened the door at the bottom of the stairs and was calling Falstaff. I immediately suspected her of plotting some terrible revenge, and that is just what she was doing.

The old Princess had no more implacable enemy than Falstaff. He was aloof, proud, and inordinately supercilious, and though he himself was devoid of love for anyone, he demanded and received everyone's proper respect, not to say fear. But suddenly, with the arrival of the old Princess in the house, all had changed; Falstaff had suffered a dreadful insult: access to the rooms upstairs was categorically denied him.

Infuriated by this affront, he had kept up a continual scratching at the door at the foot of the stairs for a whole week. But he was quick to guess who had been the cause of his banishment, and on the first Sunday that the old Princess came downstairs to go to church, Falstaff, barking and yelping, made for the poor woman. She was barely rescued from the dog's savage retaliation for her insistence that he not be allowed upstairs because she could not stand the sight of him. From that day, the most stringent measures were taken to prevent his getting upstairs, and whenever the Princess came down he was banished to a remote room.

The vindictive animal had managed nonetheless to break into the upper rooms several times. As soon as he got upstairs, he tore through the whole suite of rooms and made straight for the old Princess's bedchamber. Nothing could stop him. Fortunately, her door was always shut, and Falstaff could do no more than howl furiously in front of it, which he kept up till the servants came running and chased him downstairs. All during these visitations from the obstreperous dog, the old Princess shrieked as if she had been bitten by him, and on each occasion became ill from fear. Several times she had presented an ultimatum to her niece, and once so far forgot herself as to announce that either Falstaff or she would have to go. But the Princess refused to part with the dog.

The Princess loved Falstaff more than anyone in the world except her children, and with reason. One day, six years prior to this time, the Prince had returned from his walk bringing with him a sick, dirty, pitiful-looking little puppy, which was, however, a bulldog of the purest breed. The Prince had in some way saved the dog's life. But as this new lodger behaved in a quite gross, unseemly manner, the Princess insisted that he be consigned to the backyard, where he was kept on a rope. The Prince made no objection. Two years later, when the entire household was at a summer villa, little Sasha, Katya's younger brother, fell into the Neva. The Princess screamed, and instantly threw herself into the water after her son. Only with great difficulty was she rescued from certain death. Meanwhile, the child was being rapidly carried away by the swift current, and

117

only his clothing was visible on the surface of the water. Although they had quickly untied a boat, his rescue would have been a miracle. Suddenly the huge bulldog plunged into the water, intercepted the drowning child, grabbed him with his teeth, and triumphantly swam to shore with him. The Princess threw her arms around the wet, filthy dog and kissed him. But Falstaff, who at that time bore the prosaic and extremely plebeian name Friksa, could not bear to be caressed by anyone, and responded to the Princess's embrace by biting her shoulder as hard as he could. The Princess suffered from this injury for the rest of her life, but her gratitude was boundless notwithstanding.

Falstaff was taken into the house to live, was washed, brushed, and given an elaborately embossed silver collar. He established himself on a magnificent bearskin rug in the Princess's sitting room, and before long she was able to pet him without fear of swift and sudden reprisal. She had been horrified to learn that her pet was called Friksa, and immediately began searching for a new name, something indisputably classical. But names such as Hector and Cerberus had already become commonplace, and a name more worthy of the household favorite was required. Ultimately the Prince, with Friksa's phenomenal voracity in mind, suggested that he be called Falstaff. The suggestion was received with delight, and the name stuck.

Falstaff conducted himself very well: like a true Englishman, he was taciturn and morose, but as long as a polite detour was made around his domain on the bearskin rug and he was shown a proper respect, he never initiated an attack on anyone. Occasionally he seemed to be seized with a fit of spleen, and at such times remembered with bitterness that his enemy, the implacable enemy who had infringed on his rights, had not yet been punished. And stealthily making his way to the foot of the stairs and finding the door shut as usual, he hid in some nearby corner where he lay down and slyly waited for someone to leave the door open by mistake. Sometimes the vengeful animal waited for three days. But strict orders had been given to watch the door, and it had been two months since Falstaff had appeared upstairs.

"Falstaff! Falstaff!" called the little Princess from the stairs, opening the door and beckoning to him affably.

Sensing that the door had been opened, Falstaff was prepared to leap across his Rubicon. But it seemed so unlikely that the Princess should be calling him to come to her that he refused to believe his ears. He was as wily as a cat, and so as not to show that he had noticed the oversight of the person who had left the door open, he put his mighty paw on the windowsill and gazed out at the building opposite—in other words, behaved exactly like a stranger who had gone out for a stroll and stopped for a moment to admire the architecture of a neighboring house. Meanwhile, his heart throbbed as he reveled in sweet expectation. What was his astonishment and frantic joy when not only was the door opened wide before him but he was called, invited, implored, to go upstairs and take his just revenge without delay! He bared his teeth, and with a yelp of delight fiercely and triumphantly shot upstairs like an arrow.

The force of his momentum was so great that a chair he knocked against in flight was catapulted several feet into the air, turning over and over. Falstaff flew as if shot out of a cannon. Madame Leotard screamed in horror, but by then he had reached the sacrosanct door, and, setting upon it with his front paws, howled as if he were being slaughtered. In response there came a fearful shriek from the elderly spinster. Whole legions of his enemies converged upon him; the entire household had trooped upstairs, and Falstaff, ferocious Falstaff, with a muzzle that had been adroitly clapped over his jaws and his four feet entangled in a noose, returned ingloriously from the field of battle, dragged downstairs on the end of a rope.

An emissary was sent to the old Princess.

This time, Katya's mother was not disposed to forgive or condone the offense, but the question was: whom to punish? Her glance fell on Katya, and in the twinkling of an eye she had guessed. . . . So, it was she! Katya stood before her, pale and trembling with fear. Not until that moment had the poor girl thought of the consequences of her prank, but knowing that suspicion might fall on one of the servants, on someone who was guiltless, Katya was prepared to tell the whole truth.

"Are you to blame for this?" the Princess asked sternly.

Seeing Katya's deathly pallor I stepped forward and firmly declared: "I let Falstaff go up . . . accidentally," I added, all my courage suddenly failing me before the Princess's ominous gaze.

"Madame Leotard, see that she is properly punished!" said the Princess, and went out.

I glanced at Katya; she stood as if stunned; her arms hung limply at her sides, and her pale little face looked down at the floor.

The only punishment ever administered to the Prince's children was to shut them up in an empty room. To sit in an empty room for a couple of hours was nothing. But when the child had been confined by force, against his will, and was told that he was being deprived of his freedom, then the punishment was serious indeed. As a rule Katya or her brother was kept in the room for two hours. But in view of the enormity of my crime, I was to be shut up for four hours. Faint with joy, I went into my dungeon. I thought about the little Princess. I knew I had won a victory. But instead of four hours, it was four o'clock in the morning before I was freed. This is how it happened.

Two hours after I was locked up, Madame Leotard learned

that her daughter had arrived from Moscow, had suddenly fallen ill, and wanted to see her. Forgetting all about me, Madame Leotard went to her at once. The maid who looked after us probably assumed that I had already been let out of the room. Katya had been sent for by her mother and was obliged to remain downstairs till eleven o'clock in the evening. When she came back upstairs, she was surprised to find that I was not in bed. The maid undressed her and put her to bed, but the Princess had her reasons for not inquiring about me. She lay there waiting for me, and, knowing that my confinement was to last four hours, no doubt supposed that Nastya, our nurse, would bring me back. But Nastya too had forgotten about me, chiefly because I always undressed myself. Thus I was left to spend the night in my prison.

At four o'clock in the morning, I heard someone knocking at the door and trying to force it open. I had been sleeping, having heedlessly lain down on the floor, and on being awakened cried out in alarm. But I instantly recognized Katya's voice, which was louder than all the others, and then the voices of Madame Leotard, the frightened Nastya, and the housekeeper. At last the door was opened and Madame Leotard, with tears in her eyes, took me in her arms and begged me to forgive her for having forgotten me. I fell on her neck weeping. I was shivering with cold and my bones ached from lying on the bare floor. My eyes sought Katya, but she had run back to our bedroom and jumped into bed, and when I went into the room, she was already asleep, or pretended to be.

While waiting for me that night, she had involuntarily fallen asleep and slept till four o'clock in the morning. When she woke up, she had raised a great clamor and commotion to set me free, waking up the nurse, the maids, and Madame Leotard, who had by then returned.

By morning everyone in the house had learned of my

adventure; even Katya's mother said that they had been too severe with me. As for the Prince, that day for the first time I saw him angry. He came upstairs at ten o'clock in the morning in a state of violent agitation.

"See here," he began, addressing Madame Leotard, "what are you doing? How have you been treating this poor child? This is barbarous, absolutely barbarous—it's savagery! A weak, sick child, a dreamy, easily frightened little girl with such an active imagination—and to put her in a dark room and leave her there all night! Why, it could destroy her! Don't you know what her life has been like?.... This is barbarous, it's inhuman, I tell you, madam! How can one administer such a punishment? Who devised it—who could possibly have devised such a punishment?"

Poor Madame Leotard, mortified to tears, tried to explain what had happened, telling him that she had forgotten about me because of her daughter's arrival, that there was nothing wrong with the punishment itself, but it had simply gone on too long, and that even Jean-Jacques Rousseau speaks of something similar.

"Jean-Jacques Rousseau, madam! But Jean-Jacques Rousseau has no right to talk about this. Jean-Jacques Rousseau is not an authority, he would not dare to speak about the upbringing of children, he had no right to. Jean-Jacques Rousseau renounced his own children, madam! Jean-Jacques was an evil man!

"Jean-Jacques Rousseau! Jean-Jacques an evil man! Prince! Prince! What are you saying?"

And Madame Leotard became incensed.

She was a splendid woman, and above all reluctant to take offense, but to cast aspersions on one of her idols, to trouble the classical shades of Corneille, Racine, to insult Voltaire, to call Jean-Jacques Rousseau an evil man, a barbarian—good Heavens! Her eyes brimmed with tears, and the poor woman was so upset that she was trembling.

"You forget yourself, Prince!" she exclaimed at last, beside herself with indignation.

The Prince suddenly bethought himself and begged her pardon; then he kissed me with deep feeling, made the sign of the cross over me, and left the room.

"Pauvre prince!" said Madame Leotard, who was deeply touched in her turn.

Later we sat down at the schoolroom table, but the little Princess was extremely preoccupied. Before we went in to dinner, she came to me, all flushed and with a laugh on her lips, and taking me by the shoulders hurriedly and rather shamefacedly said:

"Well? So you took my punishment for me yesterday! . . . Let's go and play in the reception room after dinner."

Someone walked by us at that moment, and the Princess instantly turned away from me.

After dinner, at dusk, we went downstairs to the big reception room hand in hand. The little Princess was profoundly agitated and breathing heavily. I was overjoyed, happier than I had ever been before.

"Do you want to play ball?" she asked me. "Stand here."

She led me to a corner of the room, but instead of walking away and throwing the ball to me, she stopped after going a step or two, glanced at me, blushed, and falling onto the sofa buried her face in her hands. I started to go to her, but she thought I was leaving.

"Don't go, Netochka, stay with me," she said. "This will soon pass."

Suddenly she sprang up from the sofa, all flushed and tearful, and threw herself on my neck. Her cheeks were wet, her lips swollen like cherries, and her curls tossed and disheveled. She began kissing me frantically; she kissed my face, my eyes, lips, neck, and hands; she was sobbing hysterically. I pressed close to her, and we embraced sweetly and joyously like two friends, like two lovers who have met after a long separation. Katya's heart was beating so hard I could hear it.

A voice was heard in the next room summoning Katya to her mother.

"Oh, Netochka! Well, till this evening, till tonight! Go upstairs and wait for me."

Gently and silently she gave me a last, fervent kiss and ran off in response to Nastya's call. I rushed upstairs like one reborn, flung myself down on the sofa, and burying my head in the cushions sobbed with joy. My heart was beating as if it would burst my chest. I do not know how I lived till nighttime. At last the clock struck eleven and I went to bed. The Princess did not return till twelve; she smiled at me from across the room but did not speak. Nastya began to undress her and seemed to be dawdling on purpose.

"Hurry, hurry, Nastya!" murmured Katya.

"What's wrong with you, Princess, you must have run upstairs to make your heart beat so fast!" said Nastya.

"Oh, good Heavens, Nastya! How tiresome you are! Be quick, be quick!" said Katya, stamping her little foot in vexation.

"Ah, what a little darling!" said Nastya, kissing Katya's foot after she had taken off her shoe.

At last, her preparations for the night completed, the Princess was put to bed and Nastya left. Katya jumped out of bed in a flash and flung herself on me. I uttered a joyous cry.

"Come over with me, let's get into my bed!" she said, pulling me up from the bed.

A moment later I was in her bed and we embraced, eagerly pressing close to each other. Katya began kissing me almost to pieces.

"You know, I remember how you used to kiss me at night!" she said, blushing red as a poppy.

124

I sobbed.

"Netochka!" whispered Katya tearfully. "My angel, you see I've loved you for such a long, long time already! Do you know when it began?"

"When?"

"When Papa made me ask your forgiveness, and afterward you stood up for your own papa. Netochka . . . Oh, my lit-tle or-phan!" she drew out the words, again showering kisses on me. She was laughing and crying at the same time.

"Oh, Katya!"

"Well, what is it? What is it?"

"Why were we so long . . . so long . . ." but I could not go on. We clutched each other and did not speak for several minutes.

"Listen, what were you thinking about me?" asked the Princess.

"Oh, I thought so many things, Katya! I kept thinking and thinking, day and night."

"And at night you used to talk about me, I heard you."

"Really?"

"And you cried so many times!"

"No wonder! Why were you always so proud?"

"I was just stupid, Netochka. When it comes over me like that I can't do anything about it. I was awfully mean to you."

"But why?"

"Just because I was so bad. First it was because you were better than I, and after that because Papa loved you more. But Papa is a kind man, isn't he, Netochka?"

"Oh, yes!" I responded, my eyes filling with tears at the thought of the Prince.

"He's a good man," said Katya seriously, "But what am I to do about him? He's always so—— Well, and then, when I asked you to forgive me and almost started crying, that made me angry again."

"I could see it, I could see that you were ready to cry."

"Oh, be still, you little silly—you're such a crybaby yourself!" she scolded, covering my mouth with her hand. "Listen, I wanted awfully to love you, then all at once I felt like hating you, and so I hated you, just hated you!"

"But why?"

"I was angry with you. I don't know why! And later I saw you couldn't live without me, so I thought: now I'm going to torment her, the horrid girl!"

"Oh, Katya!"

"My darling!" said Katya, kissing my hand. "Well, then after that I didn't want to talk to you, I didn't want to at all. And do you remember the time I stroked Falstaff?"

"Oh, you were so fearless!"

"I-was-scared-to-death! drawled the Princess. Do you know why I did it?"

"Why?"

"Because you were watching. When I saw that you were watching me—I made up my mind to do it no matter what! I scared you, didn't I? Weren't you afraid for me?"

"Dreadfully!"

"I saw it. And wasn't I glad when Falstaff went away! Heavens! How frightened I felt afterward, when he had gone! What-a-mon-ster!"

And the Princess began to giggle nervously; then all at once she raised her hot head and began to gaze at me intently. Tears like little pearls quivered on her long eyelashes.

"But what is there about you, what made me love you so? Look at you—such a pale little thing, with your fair hair and light blue eyes, just a silly little crybaby. . . . Oh, my lit-tle or-phan!"

And Katya again leaned over and lavished kisses on me. Several of her tears fell onto my cheeks. She was deeply moved.

"And then, when I did love you, I kept thinking: no, oh no, I won't tell her! You see how stubborn I was! What was I afraid of, what was I ashamed of with you? And see how nice it is now!"

"Katya! It's so painful!" I said, in a frenzy of joy. "My heart is bursting!"

"But, Netochka! Listen to me. ... Now, listen ... who named you Netochka?"

"Mamma."

"Will you tell me everything about your mamma?"

"Everything, everything!" I replied rapturously.

"And where have you put my two lace handkerchiefs? And why did you take my ribbon? Oh, you're shameless! You see, I know!"

I laughed and blushed to tears.

"Yes, I'll torment her, I thought, just wait. And sometimes I thought: but I don't love her at all, I can't bear her. ... And you're always so meek, such a harmless little thing. And you know, I was so afraid you would think I was stupid! You're clever, Netochka, you're awfully clever, aren't you? Hm?"

"Oh, Katya, I'm not at all!" I replied, feeling almost hurt.

"Yes, you are clever," said Katya seriously and emphatically. "I know it. . . . But once I got up in the morning and I loved you so it was just awful! I had dreamed about you all night long. And I thought: I'll go and ask Mamma to let me stay downstairs with her. . . . I don't want to love her, I don't! And the next night when I was falling asleep, I thought: if I dream about her as I did last night—but then I didn't! Oh, and when I used to pretend to be asleep—— Oh, we're so shameless, Netochka!"

"But why didn't you want to love me?"

"Because ... I told you why! You see, I always loved you, always loved you! But then I couldn't bear it, I thought, I'll start kissing her sometime, or I'll pinch her to death. There now—you're such a little silly!"

And the Princess pinched me.

"And do you remember the time I tied your shoe?"

"I remember."

"And I remember; did it make you happy? I looked at you and thought: such a little dear! What would she think if I were to tie her shoe for her? And then I started feeling happy too. And, you know, I really wanted to kiss you ... but then I didn't. And afterward it began to seem so funny, so funny! The whole time we were out walking I kept feeling I would suddenly burst out laughing. I couldn't look at you it was so funny. And how glad I was that it was you who went into the dungeon instead of me!"

The empty room was called the dungeon.

"And were you scared?"

"Awfully scared!"

"But it wasn't your saying you did it that made me so happy, but that you took the punishment for me! I thought: she's crying now, but then I love her so! Tomorrow I'm going to kiss her and kiss her! And you know I wasn't sorry, really wasn't sorry for you, even though I did cry a little."

"But I didn't cry. I was specially happy."

"You didn't cry? Oh, you're wicked!" cried the Princess, sucking at my neck with her lips.

"Katya, Katya! My goodness, how pretty you are!"

"Isn't it true? Well, now what do you want with me! Torment me, pinch me! Please, pinch me! Keep pinching me, my darling!"

"Little imp!"

"And what else?"

"Little silly ..."

"And then?"

"And then kiss me!"

And, crying and laughing, we kissed each other till our lips were swollen.

"Netochka! First of all, you always have to come and sleep in my bed. Do you like kissing? We'll kiss each other. Then, I don't want you to be so unhappy. Why are you unhappy? Will you tell me? Hm?"

"I'll tell you everything. But I'm not unhappy now, I'm enjoying myself."

"Now your cheeks will be rosy, like mine!... Oh, what if tomorrow comes too soon!... Are you sleepy, Netochka?"

"No."

"Then let's talk."

And we went on chattering for hours. Heaven only knows what we talked about. First the Princess told me all about her plans for the future and how she felt about the present state of affairs. And I learned that she loved her Papa more than anyone, almost more than me. Then we both decided that Madame Leotard was very nice and not at all strict. And we went on to think out what we would do the following day, and the day after, and we settled practically everything for the next twenty years or so. Katya decided how we would live: one day she would give all the orders and I would have to carry them out, and the next day it would be my turn to tell her what to do and she would obey me implicitly; and after that we would share equally in giving orders, and in case one of us deliberately refused to obey, we would quarrel, just as a matter of form, and then quickly make up. In other words, we looked forward to everlasting happiness. Eventually we grew weary of talking, and my eyes began to close. Katya made fun of me for being a sleepyhead, but she was the first to fall asleep.

In the morning we woke up at the same time, and after a hurried kiss, I managed to get back into my own bed before anyone came in.

All that day we were so happy we hardly knew what to do with ourselves. We kept hiding, running away from everyone, and above all avoiding their eyes. Finally I began telling her about my life. Katya was shocked and moved to tears by my story.

"Oh, what a bad girl! Why didn't you tell me all this sooner? I would have loved you so——just loved you so! And did those boys on the street hurt you when they hit you?"

"Yes, and I was awfully scared of them."

"O-o-oh! They're wicked! You know, Netochka, I once saw a boy hitting another boy in the street. Tomorrow I'll take Falstaff's leash, and if we meet one of those boys, I'll give him such a thrashing!"

Her eyes flashed with indignation.

Whenever anyone came into the room we started, fearing someone might catch us kissing, and we must have kissed each other at least a hundred times that day. It was the same the next day. I was afraid I might die of joy; I was breathless with happiness. But our happiness was of short duration.

It was Madame Leotard's duty to report every move that Katya made. For three days she had been observing us, and in those three days had accumulated much to relate. Finally she went to the Princess and informed her of all she had noticed: that we were both in a frenzied state and for the past three days had been inseparable; that we had been kissing each other every moment, laughing and crying like lunatics, babbling incessantly; that since this had never been so before, she did not know what to attribute it to, but it seemed to her that the Princess was undergoing some sort of morbid crisis; and lastly, that she thought it would be better for us to see less of each other.

"I have thought so for some time," replied the Princess. "I always knew that queer little orphan would give us trouble. What they told me about her, about her former life—horrible! She has a decided influence on Katya. You say that Katya loves her very much?"

"Madly!"

The Princess flushed with vexation. She was beginning to be jealous of me on account of her daughter.

"It's unnatural," she said. "Formerly they were so incompatible, and I confess I was glad of it. However young that orphan may be, I would not vouch for her on any account. You understand me? Her breeding, her habits, and perhaps her principles were imbibed with her mother's milk. And I do not understand what the Prince sees in her. A thousand times I have suggested putting her in a boarding school."

Madame Leotard was on the point of interceding for me, but the Princess had already resolved to separate us. Katya was immediately summoned, and the moment she appeared, was told that we were not to see each other till the following Sunday, that is, for a whole week.

I learned all this late in the evening and was horror-stricken; and when I thought of Katya, I was sure that she would not be able to bear our separation. Distraught with loneliness and sorrow, I fell ill that night. In the morning, the Prince came and whispered to me to take heart. He had exerted all his influence, but to no avail: the Princess was adamant. I was gradually reduced to despair; I could scarcely draw breath I was so miserable.

On the morning of the third day, Nastya brought me a note from Katya. Penciled in a dreadful scrawl. She wrote the following:

> I love you very much. I sit here with Mamma and keep thinking about how to escape and come to you. But I will escape—I've said it, so don't cry. Write and tell me how much you love me. I'll hug you all night in my dreams. I've suffered terribly, Netochka. I'm sending you some candy. Good-bye.

I replied in the same vein and wept over Katya's note the whole day. Madame Leotard tormented me with her kindness. In the evening, I learned that she had gone to the Prince and told him that I would certainly succumb to a third illness unless I saw Katya, and that she regretted having spoken to the Princess.

I asked Nastya how Katya was and learned that she was not crying, but that she looked dreadfully pale.

In the morning Nastya whispered to me:

"Go to His Excellency's study. Go down by the stairway on the right."

Everything in me revived. Breathless with expectation, I ran downstairs and opened the door to the study. She was not there. Then suddenly I was seized from behind and Katya was kissing me eagerly. Laughter, tears. . . . In the twinkling of an eye she had broken away from my embrace, scrambled up onto her father's knees and onto his shoulders like a squirrel, then, unable to remain in that position, bounced down onto the sofa. The Prince fell down after her. She was in tears of delight.

"Papa, what a good man you are! Papa!"

"You little imps! What has happened to you two? What is this friendship, this love?"

"Hush, Papa. You don't understand our affairs."

Again we rushed into each other's arms.

I began to examine Katya more closely. She had grown thinner in those three days. The high color had faded from her little face and she looked pallid. It made me so sad I started to cry.

Eventually Nastya knocked at the door—a sign that Katya had been missed and they were asking for her. She turned deathly pale.

"Enough, children," said the Prince. "We shall see one another every day. Good-bye and God bless you."

Looking at us, he was touched; but he still erred in his reckoning. That same evening news came that little Sasha had suddenly fallen ill and was at the point of death. The Princess decided to set out the first thing in the morning. This happened so swiftly that I knew nothing about it till the very moment of saying good-bye to Katya. It was the Prince who had insisted on these farewells; the Princess all but refused to give her consent. Katya was heartbroken. I had run downstairs, beside myself, and rushed to embrace her. The traveling coach stood at the porte cochère. On seeing me, Katya uttered a scream and fainted and I flung myself on her and kissed her. Her mother tried to revive her. At last she regained consciousness and embraced me once more.

"Good-bye, Netochka!" she said to me suddenly, her face working peculiarly as she began to laugh. "Don't look at me—it's nothing—I'm not sick. I'll be back again in a month, and then we won't ever be parted again."

"Enough," said the Princess calmly. "Let us go."

But the little Princess came back once more and convulsively clasped me in her arms.

"My life!" she managed to whisper as she embraced me. "Good-bye!"

We kissed for the last time, and the little Princess vanished— for a long, long time. Eight years passed before we met again.

I have purposely recounted in detail this episode of my childhood, Katya's first appearance in my life. But our stories are inseparable: one cannot be told without the other. It seems that I was destined to meet her, that she was destined to find me. And besides, I could not deny myself the pleasure of being carried away once more by memories of my childhood. . . .

Now my story moves more rapidly. My life suddenly lapsed into a period of quiescence, and I came to myself again only after I had reached the age of sixteen.

But first, a few words about what happened to me when the Prince's family departed for Moscow.

Madame Leotard and I remained together.

Two weeks after their departure, a courier arrived from

Moscow and informed us that the return to Petersburg had been postponed indefinitely. As Madame Leotard could not go to Moscow for family reasons, her service in the Prince's house came to an end; she remained with the family, however, and moved to the home of the Princess's elder daughter, Aleksandra Mikhailovna. I have said nothing about Aleksandra Mikhailovna thus far, and, for that matter, had seen her only once. She was the Princess's daughter by her first husband. The origins and family connections of the Princess were somewhat obscure, but her first husband was known to have been a leaseholder. When the Princess remarried, she had no idea how to arrange for her daughter. A brilliant match was not to be hoped for. However, she was given a modest dowry, and four years later they succeeded in marrying her to a man who was both rich and of considerable rank. Aleksandra Mikhailovna found herself in another milieu and entered an entirely different sphere of society. The Princess visited her twice a year; the Prince, her stepfather, went to see her every week, taking Katya with him. Lately, however, the Princess had been reluctant to let Katya visit her sister, and the Prince had been taking her secretly.

Katya adored her sister. But their characters could not have been more different. Aleksandra Mikhailovna was a twenty-two-year-old woman, quiet, gentle, and loving; it was as if some secret sorrow, some hidden heartache, cast its shadow over her beautiful features. Sternness and gravity were no more in harmony with the angelic serenity of her face than mourning on a child. It was impossible to look at her without feeling profoundly sympathetic. When I first saw her, she was extremely pale, and was said to be susceptible to tuberculosis. She lived a very retired life, almost like a nun, and cared neither for social gatherings in her own home nor for going into society. She had no children at the time.

I remember her coming to see Madame Leotard, and how she

came to me and kissed me with deep feeling. She was accompanied by a thin man, no longer young, who turned out to be the violinist B. On seeing me, he shed a few tears. Aleksandra Mikhailovna put her arms around me and asked whether I would like to come and live with her and be her daughter. When I looked into her face I recognized the sister of my Katya and embraced her with a dull pain in my heart that made my whole chest ache. It was as if I had again heard someone saying: "Little orphan!"

Later Aleksandra Mikhailovna showed me a letter from the Prince. In it there were a few lines addressed to me, and I had to suppress my sobs on reading them. The Prince gave me his blessing for long life and happiness and asked me to love his other daughter. Katya also added a few lines to me. She wrote that she and her mother were now inseparable.

And so that evening I entered another family, another house with new people, and once more I was uprooted from all that had grown dear to me and to which I felt I belonged. I arrived completely exhausted and racked by heartfelt anguish. . . .

Now begins a new story.

SIX

My new life was as quiet and serene as if I had settled among hermits. I lived for more than eight years with my guardians, and in all that time I recall but few occasions when guests were invited to an evening party or dinner, when there was any sort of gathering, whether of friends, acquaintances, or relations. Except for the musician B, who was a friend of the family, two or three persons who paid an occasional visit, and those who came to see Aleksandra Mikhailovna's husband—more often than not on business—no one ever came to the house.

Aleksandra Mikhailovna's husband was constantly occupied with his business affairs and official duties. He seldom managed to find even a little free time, and when he did it was divided equally between his social life and his family. Important connections, which it was impossible for him to neglect, obliged him to make rather frequent appearances in society. There were widespread rumors concerning his boundless ambition, but as he occupied an extremely important position and enjoyed the reputation of being a serious, businesslike man, and, as good luck and success seemed to seek him out on his way, public opinion was far from denying him its sympathy. On the contrary, people always expressed a particular interest in him, which they by no means evinced for his wife. Though she lived in complete seclusion, Aleksandra Mikhailovna seemed to enjoy it. Her quiet nature was made for a life of solitude.

She became deeply attached to me and loved me like her own daughter, and with my heart still aching and my tears not yet dry after my separation from Katya, I rushed eagerly into the maternal arms of my benefactress. And from that moment my fervent love for her never wavered. She was mother, sister, friend, everything in the world to me, and took the most devoted care of me in my youth. Besides, by some instinct, some intuitive feeling, I soon sensed that her lot was by no means as happy as one might have thought on first seeing her quiet, seemingly tranquil life, her apparent ease, and the bright, serene smile that so often lit up her face. Inevitably as I began to develop, each day shed new light on something in the fate of my benefactress that was gradually and painfully divined by my heart, and along with this melancholy awareness my attachment to her grew and became stronger than ever.

Hers was a frail and timid nature. Looking at the clear, calm features of her face, one would never have imagined that any anxiety could have troubled her virtuous heart. It was unthinkable that she should be without love for anyone; compassion was always uppermost in her soul, prevailing even over revulsion, and yet she had few attachments and lived in complete solitude. Though sensitive and of a passionate temperament, she seemed to be afraid of her own feelings; it was as though she constantly stood guard over her emotions, never giving them free rein even in dreams.

Sometimes in her brightest moments I would suddenly notice tears in her eyes, as if the poignant memory of something that fretted and preyed on her conscience had unexpectedly flared up in her heart, or as if something was keeping watch over her happiness and maliciously disturbed it. It seemed that the happier she was and the calmer and more serene her life, the more likely her sudden melancholy and tears, as though this made her susceptible to an attack. I can recall not a single undisturbed month during those eight years. Her husband evidently loved her very much, and she adored him. But it seemed to me that there was something unspoken between them, some mystery in her life, or so I had begun to suspect from the very first.

Aleksandra Mikhailovna's husband made a very gloomy impression on me from the outset. This impression, formed in childhood, was never eradicated. In appearance he was tall and thin, and seemed purposely to conceal his gaze behind large green spectacles. Cold and taciturn, he had little to say even in private conversation with his wife, and he evidently found people very trying. He paid absolutely no attention to me, and consequently I was never myself on those evenings when we met for tea in the drawing room. And whenever I glanced covertly at Aleksandra Mikhailovna, I was distressed to see that even she seemed to consider every move she made. She turned pale if she noticed that her husband had become more stern and morose than usual, or suddenly blushed to the roots of her hair, as if she had heard, or suspected, an innuendo in something he had said.

I felt that it was difficult for her to be with him, yet to all appearances she could not live without him for a moment. I was struck by her extraordinary attentiveness to him, to his every word and gesture, as if she wished with all her heart to find some way to please him, yet felt she could not possibly succeed. She seemed to implore him for approval: the slightest smile on his face, the least word of tenderness, and she was happy— exactly as though these were the first moments of a still timorous, still hopeless, love. And she ministered to her husband as if he were gravely ill.

After he had left to go back to his study, always pressing Aleksandra Mikhailovna's hand and looking at her, so it seemed to me, as if her commiseration wearied him, she would change completely. Her conversation became gayer and her movements more free. But a certain discomfiture always remained with her for some time after every encounter with her husband. She invariably began recalling everything he had said, as if weighing each word. It was not unusual for her to turn to me and ask whether she had heard him aright—was it precisely thus that Pyotr Aleksandrovich had expressed himself?—as if she were searching for another meaning in his words. It was perhaps a full hour before she seemed reassured, as though she had finally succeeded in persuading herself that he had been entirely satisfied with her and there had been no cause for anxiety. Then she would suddenly become affectionate, cheerful, and happy; laughing, kissing me, or going to the piano and improvising for an hour or two. But more often than not her joy was shortlived; all at once she would start crying, and when I looked at her, troubled, bewildered, apprehensive, she was always quick to assure me—in a whisper, as if fearing we might be overheard— that her tears meant nothing, that she was quite happy, and I was not to worry about her.

There were also times when she became suddenly anxious in her husband's absence and began inquiring about him: she would send to find out what he was doing, ask the maids why orders had been given to harness the horses, where he intended to go, whether he was ill, in good spirits, or melancholy, what he had said, and so on. Apparently she herself never dared to start a conversation with him about his interests or business affairs. Whenever he gave her advice or asked her about anything, she listened to him meekly, quailing before him as if she were his slave.

She was overjoyed if he commended anything of hers, a book, her needlework, anything whatever, and it seemed to make her very proud. But her joy knew no bounds on those rare occasions when he took it into his head to fondle one of their infants (at that time they had two). Her face was transformed with happiness, and she would be completely carried away, so much so that even without any encouragement on his part she might venture to suggest—with trepidation, to be sure, and a quavering voice—that he listen to a new piece of music she had just received, or give his opinion of a new book, and she sometimes went so far as to read to him a page or two of some work that had particularly impressed her that day. At times her husband graciously acceded to these requests, smiling indulgently as one smiles at a spoiled child to whom he does not wish to deny the gratification of some strange whim for fear of harshly and prematurely thwarting him.

I do not know why, but deep in my heart I resented that smile, resented his supercilious condescension and their inequality. I restrained myself, however, and was silent, all the while intently observing them with childlike curiosity and precociously grim thoughts. At other times I noticed that he seemed to bethink himself, as though suddenly and against his will having recalled something painful, awful, and irrevocable. The condescending smile instantly vanished, and he fixed his eyes on his intimidated wife with such compassion that I winced. I realize now that had that gaze been turned on me I would have found it unbearable.

At such moments the joy faded from Aleksandra Mikhailovna's face, and the reading or the music broke off at once. She turned pale, but restrained herself and merely fell silent. There followed an awkward, oppressive moment, which sometimes seemed endless. Ultimately her husband put an end to it. Rising from his chair as if it was all he could do to suppress his agitation and annoyance, he would walk to and fro several times in sullen silence, then press his wife's hand, heave a deep sigh, and, with obvious embarrassment, murmur a few brusque words which seemed to indicate a desire to comfort her, and leave the room. Aleksandra Mikhailovna was either reduced to tears or lapsed into a prolonged and hopeless melancholy.

Often when taking his leave of her in the evening, he blessed her and made the sign of the cross over her as if she were a child, and she received his blessing with tears of gratitude and veneration.

I cannot forget certain evenings in that house (not more than two or three in the entire eight years I lived there) when Aleksandra Mikhailovna suddenly underwent a radical change. Instead of her usual self-abasement and awe of her husband, a kind of wrath or indignation was reflected in her naturally gentle face. Sometimes the storm was brewing for fully an hour: her husband became more taciturn, gloomy, and austere than ever. At last the poor woman's agonized heart could bear it no longer, and she would commence talking to him in a voice breaking with emotion, at first haltingly, disconnectedly, with vague hints and bitter allusions; then, as if unable to endure her anguish, she would give way to tears and sobbing, followed by an outburst of indignation, reproaches, recriminations, and despair—as if she had succumbed to a morbid crisis.

On these occasions it was amazing to see with what patience her husband bore it all, with what sympathy he prevailed upon her to calm herself, kissing her hands and weeping with her, till all at once she seemed to recover her self-possession as if the voice of conscience had spoken. Shaken by her husband's tears, she would wring her hands in despair, sob convulsively, and fall at his feet imploring his forgiveness, which was instantly granted. But her pangs of conscience, her tears and supplications for forgiveness, continued long afterward, and for entire months she was more intimidated and more tremulous than ever in his presence.

I understood nothing of these recriminations and reproaches; in fact, I was invariably and most inopportunely sent out of the room at such times. But they could not conceal everything from me. I was very observant, noticed certain things, and from the very beginning was imbued with a dark suspicion that some mystery lay behind all this, that these sudden outbursts of a wounded heart were not mere nervous attacks; that the husband's perpetual gloominess and his ambiguous compassion for his poor, sick wife were not without reason; that her constant timidity and trepidation before him, the meek, peculiar love she dared not show, the sudden blush or ghastly pallor in his presence, and her solitary, monastic life also had their reasons.

But such scenes with her husband were rare, and as our life was exceedingly unvarying and I was so very close to her, I gradually became accustomed to the habits and temperaments of the people I lived among. Then, too, I was growing and developing very rapidly, and much that was new, though unconscious, was awakening in me and diverting me from my observations. Of course I could not help pondering sometimes when I looked at Aleksandra Mikhailovna, but my thoughts came to nothing at the time.

I loved her deeply and respected her unhappiness, and consequently was afraid of troubling her susceptible heart with my curiosity. She understood this, and was often ready to thank me for my affection. At times, having noticed my concern, she would smile, sometimes through tears, and make fun of her tendency to cry; at other times she would suddenly begin telling me that she was very content, very happy, that everyone was so kind to her, everyone she had ever known had loved her, and that she was tormented by Pyotr Aleksandrovich's constant fretting about her and her peace of mind, when she was really so happy, so happy! And then she would embrace me with such deep feeling, and her face would radiate such love, that my heart bled, if one may so express it, with sympathy for her.

The features of her face will never be eradicated from my memory. They were regular, and her frailty and pallor seemed to accentuate the austere charm of her beauty. Her thick black hair, combed smoothly down over her ears, cast a sharp, severe shadow along the sides of her cheeks, which made an exquisite contrast with her tender glance, her large, childishly clear blue eyes, her timid smile, and that whole meek, pale face in which was reflected so much that was ingenuous, shrinking, defenseless, that was fearful of every sensation, every outburst of emotion, every momentary joy and recurrent sorrow.

Yet at certain happy, untroubled moments that heart-piercing glance was so luminous, sunny, and blessedly calm; those heavenly blue eyes radiated such love, sweetness, and profound sympathy for all that was noble, all that asked for love or compassion, that one's whole soul submitted to her, was involuntarily drawn to her, and seemed to receive from her serenity, peace of mind, reconciliation, and love. In the same way one may look at a blue sky and feel that whole hours might be spent in delightful contemplation, that the soul becomes freer and more tranquil at such times, as if the lofty dome of the firmament were reflected in it as in a still sheet of water.

When, however—and this happened often—animation brought the color to her face and her bosom heaved with emotion, then her eyes flashed like lightning and seemed to scintillate, as though the pure flame of beauty, which she had chastely guarded in her soul, had flared up in her and was reflected in those eyes. At such moments she was like one inspired. And in those unexpected outbursts of enthusiasm, in those abrupt transitions from quiet timorous moods to radiant high elation and sheer compelling rapture, there was at the same time so much naive childlike zest and belief that I think an artist would have given half his life to catch such a moment of luminous rapture and to portray on canvas that inspired face.

From my earliest days in the house I saw that she welcomed me into her solitary life. With what zest she undertook my education! She was so impetuous that, watching her, Madame

Leotard had to smile. Indeed, we tried to do everything so precipitately that we almost failed to understand one another. For instance, she set about teaching me herself, but as she began with too much at once, it resulted in more zeal, more fervor, and more loving impatience on her part than in real benefit to me.

In the beginning she was chagrined by her want of skill, but after laughing over it we made a fresh start. Undaunted by her initial failure, Aleksandra Mikhailovna courageously took issue with Madame Leotard's system. And though they laughed as they argued, my new governess flatly declared that she was opposed to any system, and insisted that by feeling our way together we would find the right path. She maintained that it was useless to stuff my head full of dry facts, and that our success would depend entirely on my instinctive understanding and her skill in stimulating my desire to learn—and she was right, as was proved by her success. In the first place, the usual pupil-teacher relation did not exist. We worked together like two friends from the very start, and sometimes, though I was unaware of the ruse, it was made to appear that I was teaching Aleksandra Mikhailovna. In fact, arguments often sprang up between us, and I became quite vehement trying to prove my point, yet all the while she was imperceptibly leading me onto the right path. When we finally arrived at the truth, I at once detected the stratagem, but when I considered all the effort she had made for me, frequently sacrificing hours in this way for my benefit, I could only throw my arms around her neck and hug her after every lesson.

My sensitivity so amazed and touched her that she was puzzled by it. Her curiosity about my past led her to question me, and after each of my recitals, she became more tender and serious with me—more serious because my unhappy childhood inspired her not so much with pity as with a certain respect. These confessions were generally followed by long conversations in which she explained my past to me, so that I actually relived it and began to understand it.

Madame Leotard often found these conversations too serious; in fact, after seeing my involuntary tears, thought them ill-advised. I was of the opposite opinion, however, because after these "lessons," I felt so relieved and satisfied that it was as though there had been nothing unfortunate in my lot. I was enormously grateful to Aleksandra Mikhailovna for making me love her more and more each day. Madame Leotard had no idea that everything which formerly had surged up in me with abnormal and precocious violence, everything which had so lacerated my young heart that it was embittered by all the unjust cruelty and cried out against the pain without knowing its source—all this was little by little being smoothed out and brought into harmony.

The day began with our visiting the nursery together to see Aleksandra Mikhailovna's infant. We tidied, dressed, and fed him, and amused ourselves by teaching him to talk. After leaving the child, we sat down to work. We applied ourselves to many subjects, but Heaven knows whether it could be called studying! It was everything without being anything definite: we would read something, discuss our impressions of it, then drop the book and turn to music, unaware of the fleeting hours. Sometimes B, who was a friend of Aleksandra Mikhailovna's, came in the evening, Madame Leotard joined us, and we had the most fervid, passionate discussions about art, life (which our little circle knew only by hearsay), about reality and ideals, the past and the future. We sometimes sat up till after midnight, and I listened to everything intently, stirred, moved, or amused along with the others. It was then that I learned all about my father and the circumstances of my early childhood.

Meanwhile, I was growing up. Teachers were engaged for me,

but without Aleksandra Mikhailovna I would have learned nothing. With the geography teacher I would only have gone blind peering at maps trying to find cities and rivers, while with Aleksandra Mikhailovna it was as if we were journeying to the countries we read about, and we saw so many marvels, experienced so many delights, spent so many fantastic hours, that in our zeal we exhausted all the books she had read and were obliged to find new ones. Before long I was able to point out things to the geography teacher, though in justice to him it must be said that he maintained his superiority over me to the very end in his thorough and precise knowledge of the latitude and longtitude on which any given city lay, and its exact population in thousands, hundreds, and even digits.

The history teacher too was dismissed in short order, and after his departure, Aleksandra Mikhailovna and I studied history in our own way; we turned to our books and were sometimes absorbed in reading far into the night, or rather, she was, for it was Aleksandra Mikhailovna who censored what was to be read. I have never experienced greater delight than after those hours of reading. We both became as exhilarated as if we ourselves were the heroes of the history we read. To be sure, we read much more between the lines than in the lines themselves, and besides, Aleksandra Mikhailovna was such a wonderful narrator that she made everything sound as if she had been present when it occurred.

It might seem ludicrous that we were so carried away that we sat up till after midnight—I a mere child, and she a wounded soul enduring life with difficulty. I know that for her it was restful to be with me. And I sometimes grew singularly thoughtful, even perceptive, as I looked at her, and before I had actually begun to live had surmised a great deal about life.

At last I turned thirteen. All during this time, Aleksandra Mikhailovna's health had been deteriorating. She grew more an] more irritable and her attacks of melancholy more severe. Though her husband spent more time with her, he was nonetheless silent, stern, and gloomy. I was very seriously worried about her.

Now that I had emerged from childhood, many new impressions, observations, interests, and conjectures were taking shape in me, and I was increasingly tormented by the enigma that seemed to exist in that family. There were times when I felt I had some understanding of the riddle; at other times, finding no solution to my questions, I lapsed into indifference, apathy, and even vexation, and my curiosity subsided. In time—and this happened more and more frequently—I felt a strange need to be alone and think, always to think. It was a period not unlike the time when I was still living with my parents but had not yet grown close to Father, when for a whole year I had pondered and reflected, peering out at the world from my corner, till I came to be like some untamed creature living in the fantasies of my own creation. The difference was that now I was more impatient, more given to yearning, to new, unconscious impulses, more eager for activity and excitement, so that to be concentrated on one thing as I had been before was no longer possible.

As for Aleksandra Mikhailovna, she seemed to withdraw from me more and more. It was hardly possible for me to be a friend to her at my age. Though I was not a child, I asked too many questions and often looked at her in a way that made her lower her eyes. There were some very strange moments. I could not bear to see her tears, and often, just looking at her, my own eyes brimmed with tears, I would throw my arms around her neck and hug her impetuously. What answer could she give me? I felt that I was a burden to her. But at other times—and those were sad and difficult moments—it was she who embraced me, convulsively and in a kind of desperation, as if unable to bear her loneliness and seeking my sympathy, as if she felt that in any case I understood her and suffered with her. But it was obvious that the mystery still stood between us, and I began to avoid her at such times. It was hard for me to be with her; besides, there was little to unite us now, apart from music. But music had been forbidden her by the doctor. Books? That was still more difficult. She was at a loss to know what to read with me. We never got beyond the first page: in every word there was the possibility of an allusion, in every insignificant phrase a hidden meaning. We both avoided intimate, personal conversations.

It was just at this time that fate, in the strangest and most extraordinary way, gave an unexpected turn to my life. My entire attention—my feelings, heart, and mind—all at once and with great intensity and fervor was suddenly directed to a different, an altogether unexpected, activity, and, without being aware of it, I was transported to a new world. I had no time to turn back, to look about me, to change my mind; although I felt that I might be going to my ruin, temptation was stronger than fear, and I shut my eyes and went ahead without thinking. And then for a long time I was diverted from the preoccupation that had begun to weigh on me, and from which I had so eagerly yet vainly sought a way out. What happened was this.

In the dining room there were three doors: one opening into the main rooms, one into the nursery and my room, and a third into the library. There was still another passage from the library, separated from my room only by a workroom where Pyotr Aleksandrovich's assistant, a man who was both secretary and overseer, was generally occupied with business correspondence. The key to the library and the bookcases was kept by him. One day after dinner, when he was not in the house, I found the key lying on the floor. Devoured by curiosity, I unlocked the door and entered the library.

It was a rather large room, very light, with eight big bookcases ranged along the walls. There were a great many books, most of which had been inherited by Pyotr Aleksandrovich, and the rest collected by Aleksandra Mikhailovna, who was continually buying books. Up to that time, the books I was given to read had been selected with such circumspection that it was not hard for me to guess that there was much that was kept from me, much that remained a mystery. Consequently, it was with irresistible curiosity and a quite singular emotion that I opened the first bookcase, which held novels, and took out my first book. Then I shut the bookcase and went back to my room with a curious sensation, a throbbing and sinking of the heart, as though I felt that some great change was about to take place in my life.

Having returned to my room, I locked the door and opened the book. But I could not read; I had something more important to do, which was to make absolutely certain of my new-found command of the library, so that no one would know of it, and I would always be able to get any book I wanted. Consequently I postponed my pleasure to a more expedient moment, took the book back to the library, and hid the key in my room. Hiding that key was the first transgression I had ever committed in my life.

I awaited the consequences, and, as it turned out, they could not have been more fortunate. Pyotr Aleksandrovich's secretary and assistant, after spending all evening and part of the night on the floor, candle in hand, searching for the key, decided in the morning to send for a locksmith. He came, bringing with him a bunch of keys, and among them one was found to fit the library door. There the matter ended, and nothing further was heard about the lost key. But I was so cautious and sly that I did not venture to go to the library again for a week, and then only when I was quite certain there was no risk of arousing suspicion. First, I chose a time when the secretary was not in the house; then I approached the library from the dining room. Pyotr Aleksandrovich's secretary always kept the key in his pocket, and having only a remote connection with the books, never went into the room where they were kept.

I began reading avidly, and before long I was completely enthralled. All my new needs, my recent aspirations, all the still vague transports of my adolescent years, and the restlessness provoked by the too early development which had created such turbulence in my soul—all this was suddenly diverted to a new outlet that had unexpectedly presented itself and, for some time, was completely satisfied with this new sustenance.

Soon my heart and mind were spellbound, and my fantasies developed to such an extent that I seemed to have forgotten the world around me. It was as though fate had brought me to the threshold of the new life to which I had been impelled and had dreamed of day and night, and before setting me on the new path had led me to the summit to show me the future in a magic panorama, a dazzling perspective.

I was destined to experience this entire future only after having read about it in books, after having experienced it in dreams, in hopes, in passionate exaltation and the sweet tumult of an adolescent heart. I began reading at random, taking the first book that came to hand; but fate watched over me: what I had learned and lived through up to that time had been so rare, so rigorous, that now I could not be enticed by anything of a diabolical or impure nature. I was saved by a child's instinct, by my tender age, and by my past.

All at once an awareness illuminated my past life. Almost every page I read was in some way familiar to me, as though I had read it long ago, as though all those passions, all that life which was now presented to me in such unfamiliar forms, in such enchanting pictures, had already been lived by me. And how fascinating it was, almost making me oblivious to the present, almost alienating me from reality, when in every book I read I found expressed the same laws of fate, the same spirit of chance, that governed the life of individual man but that derived from some fundamental law of the life of mankind and was a condition of well-being, salvation, and happiness. I exerted all my strength, all my intuition, to understand this law, of which I had a certain glimmering, and which had stirred in me a feeling that was almost self-preservation. It was as if I had had some foreknowledge of it, as if something prophetic had been brewing in my soul, fortifying my hopes. Meanwhile, I was more and more impelled toward that future, toward that life which, in my daily reading, struck me with the impact peculiar to art, casting the spell of poetry.

However, as I have already said, my fantasy prevailed over my impatience, and, indeed, only in dreams was I venturesome, while in reality I instinctively quailed before the future. And so, as if by a previous agreement with myself, I unconsciously decided to be content for the time being with the world of dreams, in which I alone was master, in which there were only temptations and joys, and where misfortune, if it were admitted at all, played only a passive, evanescent role necessary for the delicious contrasts and unexpected turns of fate that led to the happy endings of all my enthralling, imaginary romances. In retrospect, this is how I understand my mood of that period.

And to think that such a life, a life of fantasy, a life that was radically separated from all that surrounded me, could go on for three whole years!

That life was my secret, and even at the end of those three years I was in dread of its suddenly being discovered. What I had experienced during that period was too personal, too dear to me. After all, I myself was so distinctly reflected in those fantasies that I might have been frightened and confused had anyone, no matter who, cast an indiscreet glance into my soul. Then too, every member of the household lived in such seclusion, so outside of society, and in such cloistered quiet, that we had of necessity to develop inner lives of our own, to live in a kind of self-immurement. And so it was with me.

During those three years nothing changed in my surroundings; everything remained as before. A depressing monotony prevailed; when I think of it now, I believe that if I had not been immersed in my secret, hidden life, my soul would have been so tormented that I would have resorted to some unheard-of, rebellious way out of that dull, melancholy circle, and it might have been my downfall.

Madame Leotard had aged, and for the most part was confined to her room; the children were still small; B was always the same; and Aleksandra Mikhailovna's husband was as self-absorbed as ever. Between him and his wife there existed the same enigmatic relations, which seemed more and more sinister and forbidding to me, and I became increasingly alarmed for Aleksandra Mikhailovna. Her life, dreary and colorless, was being extinguished before my eyes. Every day her health grew worse. At last she seemed to despair, as if weighed down by something vague, hidden, horrifying, which, though incomprehensible to her, she accepted as the inevitable cross of a condemned life. In the end her heart was hardened by this rankling torment; even her thoughts took another direction and became dark and mournful.

I was particularly struck by one thing: I noticed that the older I grew the more estranged she was from me, till her constraint finally turned to impatient irritation. She actually seemed not to love me at certain moments, and I felt as if I were in her way. As I have said, I purposely avoided her, and once this had begun, it was as though I had been infected by her secretiveness. That is why all I had lived through during those three years, all that had taken shape in my soul in dreams, hopes, impressions, and passionate delights, I obstinately kept to myself. Once we started concealing things from each other we never became close again, although it seemed to me that I loved her more all the time.

I cannot recall without tears how deeply devoted she was, how she lavished on me all the treasures of love her heart possessed, and dedicated herself to fulfilling her vow to be a mother to me. It is true that her own sorrow sometimes distracted her attention from me for long periods of time, and she appeared to have forgotten all about me— which was not difficult, since I tried not to call attention to myself—so that as my sixteenth birthday drew near it seemed to have been quite forgotten.

In her brighter and more perceptive moments, however, Aleksandra Mikhailovna suddenly became concerned about me. She would anxiously call me away from my lessons, or whatever I happened to be occupied with in my room, shower me with questions as though testing or examining me, and remain by my side the rest of the day. She divined all my intentions and wishes, was patently worried about my present as well as my future development, and with inexhaustible love and even a certain respect tried to be of help to me. But she was by then so out of touch with me that her efforts often seemed naive, and were quite transparent to me.

For instance—and this happened when I was sixteen—she interrupted me one day to ask what I was reading, and was appalled when she learned that I had not yet gone beyond children's literature for twelve-year-olds. I guessed what was in

153

her mind and observed her closely. For the next two weeks she appeared to be preparing and testing me, trying to determine the degree of my development and my needs. At last she decided to make a start, and Sir Walter Scott's novel *Ivanhoe* appeared on our table—a book I had long since read at least three times.

At first she studied my reactions with anxious expectation, as if weighing them with misgivings. Eventually the constraint that had existed between us, and of which I was very aware, disappeared. We were both exhilarated, and I was glad, so very glad, that I no longer had to hide my feelings from her. When we finished the novel she was delighted with me. Every observation I had made during our reading was sound, every impression true. To her mind, I had developed tremendously. She was so pleased with me that in her elation—and also because she did not want to be separated from me any longer—she was prepared to undertake the supervision of my education again; but this was not in her power. Fate soon separated us once more and impeded our friendship. It took no more than an attack of illness and one of her usual fits of melancholy for the estrangement, secretiveness, mistrust, and even a certain bitterness to recur.

But even during those times there were moments over which we had no control. Reading together, or over music, or after exchanging a few sympathetic words, we would forget ourselves and speak freely, sometimes even too freely, whereupon we became ill at ease. Having bethought ourselves, we would look at each other in dismay, with suspicion, curiosity, and mistrust. For both of us there was a limit to the intimacy we could permit ourselves, and beyond which we dared not go, however much we might have wanted to.

One day, just before dusk, I was dreaming over a book in Aleksandra Mikhailovna's sitting room. She was at the piano improvising on a theme from one of her favorite Italian operas. When she came to the pure melody of the aria, I was so captivated by the music, which had moved me profoundly, that I began timidly, in a low voice, humming the melody to myself. Soon I was completely carried away, and rose and moved to the piano. Just as if she had expected me, Aleksandra Mikhailovna began playing the accompaniment, sensitively following every note as I sang. She seemed to be amazed by the resonance of my voice. I had never sung in her presence before, and hardly knew myself whether I had a voice. Suddenly we were both inspired. My voice continued to rise as I anticipated every measure of her accompaniment; energy and passion were awakened in me, kindling her admiration still more. The song ended so triumphantly, with such spirit and power, that she seized my hands and gazed at me with delight.

"Anneta! Why, you have a wonderful voice!" she said. "Good heavens! How could I have failed to notice it?"

"I myself was not aware of it till just now," I replied, beside myself with joy.

"God has blessed you, my dear, precious child! Thank Him for this gift. Who knows . . . Oh, my God! My God!"

She was so moved and astonished, so ecstatically happy, that she did not know what to say to me, how to express her feelings. It was one of those moments of revelation, of mutual sympathy and closeness, that we had not known for a long time.

An hour later it was as if a holiday were being celebrated in the house. B was immediately sent for. While waiting for him to come, we chanced to discover another piece of music that was more familiar to me, and launched into another aria. This time I was trembling with apprehension; I did not want to destroy the first impression by a failure. My voice soon gathered strength, however, and I felt reassured. I myself was more and more astonished at its power, and during this second experiment all doubt was dispelled.

In her impetuous joy, Aleksandra Mikhailovna sent for her children, their nurse, and was even so rash as to call her husband away from his study, which as a rule she would not have dreamed of doing.

Pyotr Aleksandrovich listened to her news benevolently, congratulated me, and was the first to declare that I must be given lessons. Aleksandra Mikhailovna was as overcome with gratitude as if he had done something unheard-of for her, and she rushed to kiss his hand.

At last B arrived. He too was overjoyed, for he loved me very much. He still remembered Father and the past. After hearing me sing two or three songs, he announced with a serious, preoccupied air that I unquestionably had ability, perhaps even talent, and that it would be inconceivable not to give me lessons. Afterward, as if thinking better of their enthusiasm, he and Aleksandra Mikhailovna both expressed the opinion that it would be dangerous to praise me prematurely. I noticed, however, that they instantly exchanged winks and were secretly in agreement, so that all their talk about not praising me was rather lame and transparent.

I had to laugh to myself all evening as I watched them trying to restrain themselves and making deliberate and audible remarks about my shortcomings after each new song. But they could not keep it up for long; B himself was the first to give in and was again carried away by his joy. I had never suspected that he loved me so much.

The whole evening was spent in the warmest, most amicable conversation. B related the histories of several celebrated singers and actors, speaking with the enthusiasm of an artist, reverently and with emotion. My father having been mentioned, the conversation turned on me and my childhood, then shifted to the Prince and the members of his family, about whom I had heard very little since parting from them. Aleksandra Mikhailovna herself knew little or nothing about them. As he frequently went to Moscow, B knew more than anyone. At that point the conversation took a rather mysterious, puzzling turn, and two or three particulars relating to the Prince were incomprehensible to me.

Aleksandra Mikhailovna mentioned Katya, but B could tell us almost nothing about her, indeed, he gave the impression of being definitely reluctant to speak of her. This surprised me. Not only had I not forgotten Katya, not only was I unable to stifle my former love for her, but I did not for one moment think there could be any change in her. I was oblivious of our separation, of the long years we had lived apart, during which there had been no correspondence between us, and of the differences in our upbringing and character. In my mind, after all, Katya had never left me; she still seemed to exist within me, especially in my dreams, in all the romances and adventures of my fantasies, where we walked hand in hand, always together. I imagined myself the heroine of every novel I read and always put Katya, my princess-friend, into the story with me. Every novel had two parts, of course, one of which was created by me, with shameless borrowings from my favorite authors.

It was finally decided in the family council to engage a singing teacher for me. B recommended the best and most famous one. The following day the Italian, D, appeared. He listened to me, concurred in the opinion of his friend B, but declared that I would benefit greatly by going to him for my lessons, where I could study with his other pupils, and where the competition, emulation, and wealth of resources at my disposal would be advantageous for the development of my voice. Aleksandra Mikhailovna gave her consent, and from then on, between eight and nine o'clock in the morning on three days a week, I would set out for the conservatory accompanied by one of the servants.

I shall now recount a certain strange occurrence which had a decisive influence on me and was a turning point in my life. I was sixteen years old at the time, and suddenly an inexplicable apathy came over me; I was afflicted with an unbearable, depressing lethargy which I myself could not understand. All my fantasies and enthusiasms subsided, my daydreaming suddenly waned from lack of vitality, and my former youthful fervor was replaced by cold indifference. Even my talent, about which everyone I loved had been so enthusiastic, was devoid of interest for me and I listlessly neglected it. Nothing diverted me; my coldness and indifference extended even to Aleksandra Mikhailovna, and for this I reproached myself, as I could not help being conscious of it.

My apathy was brought to an end by unforeseen tears and an inconceivable sorrow, and once again I sought solitude. At that very strange time, a singular occurrence shook me to the depths of my being, and transformed what had been a lull into a genuine storm. I was heart-stricken.

This is how it came about. . .

SEVEN

I went into the library (that will be an eternally unforgettable moment for me) and took down *St. Ronan's Well,* the only one of Sir Walter Scott's novels I had not yet read. I remember that a vague, tormenting anguish had been haunting me like a premonition. I felt like crying. The room was bright, lit by the slanting rays of the setting sun, which streamed through the high windows and fell across the gleaming parquet floors. It was quiet; there was not a soul in the adjoining rooms. Pyotr Aleksandrovich was not at home and Aleksandra Mikhailovna was ill and confined to her bed. I was actually crying when I opened the second part of the book and leafed aimlessly through it, looking for something meaningful in phrases that caught my eye. It was like telling one's fortune by opening a book at random and reading the first thing one happens to see.

There are moments when all our mental and emotional powers are acutely heightened and seem suddenly to blaze with the bright flame of consciousness. At such times, as if overwhelmed by a presentiment, a foretaste of the future, something prophetic is envisioned by the astonished soul, and one's whole being longs to live, cries out to live, and the heart, inflamed with a blind, fervent hope, invokes the future, despite its mystery and incertitude, its storms and tempests, if only it be life. It was just such a moment for me.

I recall that I had shut the book with the intention of

opening it again at random with my future in mind and reading whatever my eyes happened to fall on. But when I opened it, I saw a sheet of letter paper folded in four and covered with handwriting. The paper had become so flat and dry that it must have been slipped between the pages of the book years ago and forgotten. I began to examine my discovery with the greatest curiosity. It was not addressed to anyone and was signed with the initials "S.O." My interest was redoubled. I unfolded the paper, which was almost stuck together and had lain so long in the book that a light square was outlined on the discolored pages. The folds of the paper were worn and cracked, and it was obvious that at one time it had been read often and saved as something very precious. The ink was faded and bluish—the letter evidently had been written years ago.

Several words that caught my eye made my heart beat rapidly in expectation. Confused, I turned the letter over in my hands as if purposely postponing the moment of reading it. I happened to hold it up to the light; yes, tears had fallen on those lines and spotted the paper; here and there whole characters were obliterated by teardrops. Whose were those tears? At last, faint with expectation, I read half of the first page—and uttered an involuntary cry of astonishment. I locked the bookcase, returned the key to its place, and having concealed the letter in my kerchief ran to my room, locked the door, and began to read it again from the beginning. But my heart was pounding so that the words flickered and danced before my eyes. It was some time before I could make anything out. The letter was a revelation. I realized in a flash that it contained the heart of a mystery, for I had discovered to whom it had been written. I knew that I was almost committing a crime in reading that letter, but the moment was too much for me. The letter was to Aleksandra Mikhailovna.

I shall quote it here. At first I but dimly realized what it contained, but later the solution to the riddle weighed long and

160

heavily on my mind. From that moment my life was shattered. My heart was agitated and perturbed for a very long time, virtually forever, because the letter itself evoked so much in me. Truly, I had looked into the future.

It was a farewell letter, awful in its finality. After reading it, I was heartsick, as if I myself had lost everything and was bereft forever of even my hopes and dreams, as if nothing were left to me but useless life. Who was he, the author of this letter? And what had her life been afterward? There were so many allusions, so many particulars, in the letter that it was impossible to be mistaken, yet there were also so many riddles that it was equally impossible not to become lost in conjecture. But I could hardly be mistaken; to say nothing of the tone of the letter, which implied so much, its content revealed the whole character of a relationship in which two hearts had been broken. The thoughts and feelings of the writer were exposed. They were extremely personal, and, as I have said, prompted one to conjecture. But here is the letter, copied word for word:

"You said you would not forget me—I believe you, and henceforth my entire life is in those words of yours. We must part: the hour has struck for us! I knew this long ago, my sad and gentle lovely one, but only now have understood it. During all this time that you have loved me, my heart has ached and grieved for our love, and now—can you believe it?—I feel relieved! I have long known that this is how it would end, that this was ordained for us from the first. It is fate! Listen to me, Aleksandra: I was not your *equal*, I have always, *always* felt this. I was not worthy of you, and I, I alone, should have borne the penalty for my lost happiness. Tell me, what was I compared to you when you first knew me? God! Two years have passed already, and all that time I was practically unconscious; I was incapable of realizing till now that *you* loved *me!* I cannot understand how it ever came about, how it began. Do you remember what I was compared to you? In what way was I

161

worthy of you, how could I have attracted you, what was particularly remarkable about me? Until you came into my life, I was coarse and simple, with a lugubrious, sullen look. I had no desire for a different life, gave no thought to it, neither asked for it nor looked for it. Everything in me was somehow crushed, and I knew of nothing in the world more important than my commonplace, routine work. I had only one concern—tomorrow—and was indifferent even to that. At one time—but that was long ago—I imagined something like this, and used to dream like a fool. But time passed, and I had long since begun to live a calm, lonely, austere life, not even feeling the cold that was turning my heart to ice as it fell into a long slumber. You see, I knew, I had made up my mind, that the sun would never rise for me again; I believe this and did not complain about anything, because I knew that that was how it *had to be*.

"When you passed by me, I did not dare to raise my eyes to you. I was a slave compared to you. My heart did not tremble when I was near you, did not ache and pine for you: it was untroubled. My soul did not perceive yours, though it shone beside its beautiful sister. This I know and have dimly felt. And I could feel it because the morning sun sheds its light on the least blade of grass, warms and nurtures it as it does the most superb flower that grows next to it.

"But then when I realized everything—you remember, after that evening, after those words that shook me to the depth of my soul—I was dazzled, staggered, everything in me was seething, and, do you know, I was so thunderstruck that I did not trust myself, and did not understand you! I have never talked to you about this. You knew nothing about it; in the past I was not the same as I was when you found me. If I could have spoken, and had dared to speak, I would have confessed everything to you long ago. But I was silent, and now I tell you everything so that you may know who it is you are leaving, the

162

kind of man you are parting from.

"Do you know when I began to understand you? Passion had consumed me like fire, like poison it flowed in my blood, stirring up my thoughts and feelings; I was drunk, in a daze, and responded to your pure, *compassionate* love not as if I were your equal, not as if I were worthy of your pure love, but insensibly, heartlessly. I did not understand you. I replied to you as to one who was oblivious of me, and not as to one who wanted to raise me to her level. Do you know what I suspected you of, what 'oblivious of me' meant to me? I will not insult you with my confession; I will tell you only one thing: you were bitterly mistaken in me! Never, never could I have risen to your level. I could only contemplate you from afar, with infinite love, after I had understood you, but this did not expiate my guilt. The passion you aroused in me was not love—I was afraid of love; I did not dare to love you; in love there is reciprocity, equality, which I was not worthy of.... I don't even know what was wrong with me. Oh, how can I tell you, how can I make myself understood?.... In the beginning I did not believe—— Oh, do you remember when my first excitement subsided, when my vision cleared, when there remained an absolutely pure, chaste feeling? My first reaction was one of surprise, confusion, fear, and do you remember how I suddenly fell at your feet sobbing? And do you remember how, embarrassed, aghast, and with tears in your eyes, you asked me what was the matter with me? I was silent, I could not answer you; but my soul was torn apart; my happiness crushed me, it was suddenly unbearable, and my sobs spoke within me: 'Why has this happened to me? What have I done to deserve it? What have I done to be worthy of this bliss?' My sister, my sister! Oh, how many times—you did not know this—how many times I secretly kissed your dress, but secretly, because I knew I was unworthy of you, it took my breath away, and my heart beat so hard, so slowly, that I thought it would stop altogether and never beat again.

"When I took your hand I was pale and trembling; your pure soul disconcerted me. Oh, I cannot tell you all that has accumulated in my heart and is longing to be expressed! Do you know that your constant, compassionate tenderness was at times painful and distressing to me? When you kissed me (it happened only once and I will never forget it), there was a mist before my eyes and my heart stood still. Why did I not die at your feet at that moment?

"I am addressing you in the intimate form for the first time, though you asked me to do so long ago. Can you understand what I am trying to say? I want to tell you *everything,* and I will say this: Yes, you loved me very much; you loved me as a sister loves a brother; you loved me as your own creation, because you resurrected my heart, you awakened my mind from its slumber, and filled my breast with sweet hope. But I could not, dared not, call you my sister till now, because I could not be your brother, because I was not your equal, because you were deceived in me.

"But you see, I am writing everything about myself; even now, at this moment of terrible calamity, I think only of myself, though I know that you are worrying about me. Oh, don't worry about me, dear friend! If you knew how debased I am in my own eyes! You will be rejected because of me, scorned and jeered at because I stand so low in their opinion. Oh, how guilty I am for not being worthy of you! If only I were of some consequence, of some worth in their eyes, and inspired them with more respect, then they might forgive you! But I am inferior, I am insignificant, I am ridiculous, and there can be nothing lower than to be ridiculous. After all, who is it that cries out? It is just because *they* have already begun to raise their voices that I have lost courage; I was always weak. You understand the position I am in: I have to laugh at myself, and I believe they are right, because I am ridiculous and odious even to myself. I feel this because I despise my face, my form, every habit and ignoble mannerism; I have always despised them! Oh, forgive me for my crude despair! It is you who taught me to say everything to you. I have been your undoing, I have brought malice and ridicule upon you because I was unworthy of you.

"And it is this very thought that plagues me, that pounds in my head incessantly, that wounds and racks my heart. And it has always seemed to me that you loved the man you thought to find in me, but that you had deceived yourself. This is what now torments me and will go on tormenting me to the day I die, or till I go out of my mind.

"And so, good-bye, good-bye! Now, when all has come to light, when their cries have been raised, their gossip heard (I have heard it!), when I have been debased, humiliated in my own eyes, ashamed even for you because of your choice, when I have cursed myself—now I must run away, disappear, for the sake of your peace of mind. This is what they require. And you will never, never see me again! So it must be; so it is destined to be!

"Too much was given to me; fate made an error, and now she is correcting it and taking everything back. We met, we knew each other, and now we part till we meet somewhere else! Where will it be, where will it be? Oh, tell me, my darling, where we shall meet again. Where shall I find you, and will we know each other then? My soul is completely permeated with you. Oh, why, why has this happened to us? Why do we part? Teach me—I cannot understand this, will never in any way understand it—teach me how to tear my life in two, how to tear the heart out of my breast and live without it. Oh, I will be haunted always by the thought that I am never to see you again, never, never!. . .

"God! What an outcry they have raised! How fearful I am for you now! I have just seen your husband; we are both unworthy of him, though we are guiltless before him. He knows every-thing, he sees it all and understands us. It was as clear as day to him from the first. He stood up for you heroically; he will save you; he will defend you against their gossip, against the hue and cry; he has boundless love and respect for you. He is your savior, whereas I run away! I rushed to him, I wanted to kiss his hand. He told me that I was to leave without delay. It is settled! They say that he has quarreled with all of them because of you; they were all against you! They reproach him with indulgence and weakness. My God! What more will they say about you? They do not know, *they cannot know, they are incapable of understanding!* Forgive them, my poor darling, as I forgive them; they have taken more away from me than from you!

"I am beside myself, I do not know what I am writing to you. What did I say to you yesterday when we parted? You see, I have forgotten everything. I was distracted—you were crying. . . . Forgive me for those tears! I am so weak, so cowardly!

"There was something else I wanted to say to you. . . . Oh, if only my tears could fall upon your hands again as they now fall on this letter! Once more to be at your feet! If *they* but knew how noble your feelings were! But they are blind; their hearts are proud and arrogant; they do not see and will never see this. They see *nothing!* They will not believe that you are innocent, even according to their judgment, though everything on the face of the earth were to testify to it. As if they could understand this! How can they cast a stone at you? Whose was the first hand to pick up a stone? Oh, they have no qualms, they will cast a thousand stones because that is something they know how to do! If it were only possible to tell them everything candidly, so they might see, hear, understand, and believe!. . . But no, they are not that wicked. Being now in despair, I perhaps malign them. And I may frighten you with my fear. Do not be afraid, do not fear them, my darling! They will understand you; after all, one of them already understands you. Take heart: that one is your husband!

"Farewell, farewell! *I do not thank you!* Farewell forever!

"S.O."

My confusion was so great that for some time I could not understand what had happened to me. I was shocked and frightened. Reality had taken me by surprise in the midst of the simple life of dreams in which I had spent three years. I was frightened to feel that I held a great mystery in my hands, and that this mystery was now linked to my whole existence. . . . But how? That I did not know. I felt at that moment that a new life was beginning for me. I had become an unwitting participant, and far too deeply implicated, in the lives and personal relations of those who up to that time had made up my whole world, and I became fearful for myself. Why should I, an outsider, enter into that life unbidden? What could I bring to them? What sanction was there for this unexpected involvement in another's secret life? Who could tell, perhaps my new role would be distressing both to me and to them? Yet I could not remain silent, could not refuse to accept this role and seal up what I knew irrevocably in my heart. What would be the result for me? What should I do? And what, after all, had I found out? Thousands of questions, still vague and confused, rose in my mind and became unbearably oppressive. I felt bewildered.

Later, I recall, I had moments in which my impressions were quite strange and different from anything I had ever experienced before. I felt as though something had been resolved within me, that my former depression had suddenly dropped away from me and something new had begun to take its place—something over which I still did not know whether to grieve or rejoice. What I was going through at that time was

167

comparable to the experience of a man who, as he leaves forever the home where he has led a calm, untroubled life, sets out on a long journey to an unknown region, and before departing looks about him for the last time, mentally saying farewell to his past, sick at heart and full of misgivings about the unknown, perhaps harsh and hostile, future that awaits him.

Finally convulsive sobs broke from me, and my heart was torn with anguish. I had to see and hear someone, had to hold someone in close embrace. I could no longer remain by myself; I rushed to Aleksandra Mikhailovna and spent the whole evening with her. We were alone. I asked her not to play the piano, and I refused to sing although she asked me. Everything had become so difficult and I was unable to fix my mind on anything. I believe we both cried. I remember only that she became quite alarmed about me and tried to persuade me to calm myself and not be so perturbed. She observed me with dismay, insisting that I was ill and not taking care of myself. At last I left her; I was completely worn out and distraught and went to bed in a feverish state, almost as if delirious.

Several days passed, during which I was able to recover my self-possession and consider my position more clearly. Aleksandra Mikhailovna and I were living in complete solitude at the time, Pyotr Aleksandrovich having gone to Moscow on business, where he remained for three weeks. Despite the briefness of their separation, Aleksandra Mikhailovna fell into a state of deep despondency. There were times when she was more composed, but she shut herself up in her room nonetheless, and even my presence was irksome to her. Besides, I myself was seeking solitude. My mind was working constantly and I was under a severe strain. I was more or less in a daze. Sometimes for long hours I was in the throes of harassing, obsessive thought; then I imagined that someone was slyly mocking me; it was as though there were something in me that confused and poisoned my mind. I could not get rid of the tormenting images that rose before me at every moment and gave me no peace. I envisaged long, hopeless suffering, martyrdom, my abject, stoical, unavailing sacrifice, and saw the one for whom the sacrifice was made scorning and deriding it. I seemed to see a criminal pardoning the sins of one who was righteous, and my heart was lacerated. . . . At the same time, I longed to rid myself of my suspicion; I cursed it, despised myself because all my convictions were less convictions than presentiments, and because I could not justify them to myself.

I mentally reviewed all those phrases, those last terrible cries of farewell. I pictured to myself that man who was *not her equal,* tried to fathom the whole agonizing significance of those words " *not equal.* " I was poignantly struck by that despairing farewell: "I am ridiculous, and am ashamed even for you because of your choice . . ." What did it mean? Who were they? Why were they lamenting, what tormented them, what had they lost? Composing myself, I tensely reread the letter, in which there was so much despair and remorse, the meaning of which was strange and and incomprehensible to me. But the letter fell from my hands and my heart was increasingly possessed by nervous agitation. . . . All this had to be resolved somehow, but either I could see no way out, or if I could, dreaded it!

I was virtually ill by the time a carriage rumbled into our courtyard one day bringing Pyotr Aleksandrovich back from Moscow. Aleksandra Mikhailovna ran to meet her husband with a cry of joy, but I was incapable of moving. I remember being alarmed by my own unexpected emotion.

A quarter of an hour later I was sent for and given a letter from the Prince. In the drawing room I met a stranger who had come from Moscow with Pyotr Aleksandrovich and, from what

I gathered, intended to remain with us for some time. He was the Prince's agent, and he was here in Petersburg to take care of certain important family affairs which had long been under Pyotr Aleksandrovich's administration.

When he gave me the letter from the Prince, he said that the young Princess had also meant to write and had assured him up to the very last minute that the letter would be ready for him to take, but in the end had let him go emptyhanded. He was to tell me that there was simply nothing to write as nothing could be said in a letter; that she had spoiled at least five sheets of letter paper and then torn them up; that in any case our friendship would have to be renewed before we could write to each other. Afterward she had told him to assure me that we would soon meet again. In reply to my eager questions, he said that an early meeting was quite certain, as the whole family would arrive in Petersburg before long.

I could hardly contain my joy at this news, and hastily went to my room, locked myself in, and tearfully opened the Prince's letter. In it he promised that I would soon see both him and Katya, and, with deep feeling, congratulated me on my talent. At the end of the letter, he promised to make all the necessary arrangements for my future, and gave me his blessing.

I wept as I read this, but mingled with my sweet tears there was such unbearable sadness that I remember feeling worried about myself. I did not know what was happening to me.

In the room next to mine, which had formerly been the office of Pyotr Aleksandrovich's secretary, the new arrival now worked every morning and often in the evening till midnight. Sometimes he and Pyotr Aleksandrovich shut themselves up in the study to work. One day Aleksandra Mikhailovna asked me to go to her husband's study and inquire whether he would care to join us for tea. Finding no one in the study, and supposing that Pyotr Aleksandrovich would return soon, I decided to wait. His portrait hung on the wall. I remember shuddering when I caught sight of that portrait, but then I began to examine it intently and with an agitation that I myself could not understand. It hung rather high on the wall, and as it was quite dark in the room I had to stand on a chair in order to scrutinize it more closely. I was searching for something in it, as though hoping to find a solution to my doubts. I recall being struck first by the eyes. I suddenly realized that I had never seen the man's eyes: they were always hidden behind spectacles.

For some obscure, incomprehensible reason I had not liked that look even as a child, and now my prejudice seemed justified. My imagination was stirred. All at once it seemed to me that the eyes in the portrait looked away from my probing, questioning gaze, that they were trying to avoid it, that there was hypocrisy and deceit in those eyes. I felt that I had guessed the truth, and a mysterious joy sprang up in me as a result of my perspicacity. A faint cry escaped me.

At that moment I heard a rustling sound behind me. I looked around: there stood Pyotr Aleksandrovich looking at me attentively. It seemed to me that he turned suddenly crimson. I blushed and jumped down from the chair.

"What are you doing here?" he asked sternly. "Why are you in this room?"

I did not know what to reply. After making some slight excuse, I gave him Aleksandra Mikhailovna's message. I cannot remember his answer, nor how I managed to get out of the room. When I returned to Aleksandra Mikhailovna I had completely forgotten what he had said and, hazarding a guess, told her that he would come to tea.

"But what is the matter, Netochka?" she asked. "Your face is all flushed; look at yourself. What is it?"

"I don't know . . . I was hurrying . . ." I replied.

"What did Pyotr Aleksandrovich say to you?" she asked in confusion.

I made no reply.

At that moment we heard his footsteps, and I hastily left the room. For two hours I waited in great anxiety. At last I was summoned to Aleksandra Mikhailovna. She was reticent and preoccupied. As I entered the room, she darted a searching glance at me and instantly lowered her eyes. She appeared to be disconcerted. I noticed that she was not in a good mood, scarcely spoke, and avoided looking at me. In reply to B's solicitous questions, she complained of a headache. Pyotr Aleksandrovich was more talkative than usual, but spoke only to B.

Aleksandra Mikhailovna went to the piano with a preoccupied air.

"Sing something for us," said B, turning to me.

"Yes, Anneta, sing your new aria," Aleksandra Mikhailovna was quick to add, as if delighted with the proposal.

I glanced at her; she was looking at me with anxious expectation.

But I was not in control of myself; instead of going to the piano and somehow getting through a song, I became flustered and embarrassed and did not know how to excuse myself. In the end my discomfiture prevailed and I refused outright.

"Why don't you want to sing?" asked Aleksandra Mikhailovna, looking at me significantly after darting a glance at her husband.

These two glances provoked me. In extreme confusion, which I could no longer conceal, I rose from the table and, trembling with uncontrollable irritation, hotly repeated that I did not wish to sing, and could not in any case because I was not feeling well. Having spoken, I looked everyone straight in the eye, though, God knows, at that moment all I wanted was to escape from them all and hide in my room.

B was astounded, and Aleksandra Mikhailovna, who became visibly distressed, was speechless. Pyotr Aleksandrovich instantly rose from his chair saying that he had forgotten about a certain business matter, and, evidently vexed at having wasted valuable time, hurriedly left the drawing room murmuring something about dropping in later. He shook hands with B, however, which indicated that he had no intention of returning.

"Just what is the matter?" B asked me. "You really do look ill."

"Yes, I am—I'm feeling quite ill," I replied impetuously.

"Indeed, you're quite pale, and only a little while ago you were so flushed," remarked Aleksandra Mikhailovna and stopped abruptly.

"That's enough!" I said, going straight up to her and looking into her face intently.

The poor woman could not bear my look and lowered her eyes guiltily. A slight flush suffused her cheeks. I took her hand and kissed it, and she looked at me with naive, unfeigned joy.

"Forgive me for being such a bad, ill-tempered child today," I said to her with feeling, "but really . . . I am ill. Don't be angry with me, and let me go now."

"We are all children," she said with a timid smile. "Even I am a child, and worse, much worse than you," she whispered in my ear. "Go now, and be well. Only, for Heaven's sake, don't be angry with me."

"What for?" I asked, astonished at such an ingenuous confession.

"What for . . ." she repeated, in great confusion, as if, in fact, she felt apprehensive. "What for?" Well, you will see what sort of person I am, Netochka. What was it I said to you?. . . Well, *adieu!* You are cleverer than I. . . . And I am worse than a child."

"Come, that's enough!" I said, deeply moved and not knowing what to say.

I kissed her once more and hurriedly left the room. I was terribly perturbed and dejected. Moreover, I was vexed with myself, feeling that I was imprudent and did not know how to conduct myself. Mortified to tears, I went to bed in a state of deep depression.

When I woke up in the morning my first thought was that the whole evening had been pure illusion, a mirage, that we had simply been mystifying one another, had been in too great a hurry to make a mountain out of a molehill, and that all this came from inexperience and our habit of not accepting the outward aspect of things. I felt that the letter was to blame for everything, that I had been too upset by it because of my disordered imagination, and I decided that in future I would do better not to think about things. Having resolved all my anguish with such remarkable ease, and fully persuaded that I could with equal ease carry out what I had resolved, I went off to my singing lesson quite cheerfully and the morning air cleared my head.

I loved the morning excursion to my teacher. It was delightful to walk through the city, which by eight o'clock was quite animated and filled with people briskly setting about their daily activities. We usually passed through the same lively, narrow little streets. It pleased me that my artistic life was beginning in such surroundings. I like the contrast between the minutiae of everyday life with its small but vital cares and that art which awaited me only a few steps from it on the third floor of an immense house filled with lodgers who had nothing whatever to do with art. I walked among those busy, cross-looking people, with my music under my arm, and could not help wondering what old Natalya, who always accompanied me, was thinking. And then there was my teacher, an eccentric man, half-Italian, half-French, who was at times a genuine enthusiast, more often a pedant, and above all a miser, which amused me and either made me laugh or led me to ponder. And though I was unsure of myself, I loved my art with passionate hope, built castles in the air, and envisaged a wonderful future for myself. I often returned home aglow with fantasies, and during these hours was almost happy.

I was caught up in just such a moment when I returned home one day at ten o'clock, lost in dreams, unmindful of everything about me. As I mounted the stairs, I suddenly started as if I had been scalded. I had heard the voice of Pyotr Aleksandrovich, who was at that moment coming down. The disagreeable sensation that came over me was so powerful, and my recollection of what had occurred the previous day filled me with such antagonism, that I could not conceal my distress. I bowed slightly to him, but my face must clearly have revealed what I felt at the moment because he stopped before me in surprise. I blushed and quickly went upstairs. He muttered something as I passed and continued on his way.

I was ready to weep with vexation and could not understand why this had happened. I was not myself all morning and was unable to decide how to put an end to all this, how to be rid of it as quickly as possible. A thousand times I promised myself to be more reasonable, and a thousand times fear got the better of me. I felt that I hated Aleksandra Mikhailovna's husband, and at the same time was in despair over myself. I was actually unwell from the ceaseless agitation and could not control myself. Everything irritated me, and I spent the whole morning in my room, not even going to see Aleksandra Mikhailovna. Finally she came to my room, and almost cried when she saw me. I was so pale that I myself was alarmed when I looked into a mirror. Aleksandra Mikhailovna remained with me for an hour, waiting on me as if I were a baby.

But her kindness and concern made me so miserable, and it was so painful for me to look at her, that in the end I asked her to leave me alone. She left in a state of great anxiety. At last my anguish found relief in weeping. By evening I felt better.

The reason I felt better was that I had decided to go to her, to fall on my knees before her, give her the letter she had lost, and confess everything: all the torments I had endured and all my doubts. I would embrace her with the infinite love that burned in me for her, my martyr, tell her that I was her child, her friend, let her look into my heart so she could see my fervent, steadfast feeling for her. My God! I felt that I was the last person to whom she could open her heart, but the more persuasive my words, the more certain her salvation. Although I understood her sorrow in a dim, confused way, my heart seethed with indignation at the thought of her blushing before me, before my judgment. . . . My poor, poor friend, can that sinner have been you? That is what I would say to her, after weeping at her feet. . . . My sense of justice was outraged, and I became incensed.

I do not know what I might have done, but I had no sooner regained my self-possession than an unforeseen occurrence saved both her and me from ruin. I was aghast. Could her tortured heart ever have risen to hope again? I might have killed her at one stroke.

What happened was this: when I was but two rooms away from her sitting room, Pyotr Aleksandrovich appeared coming through a side door and, not seeing me, proceeded on his way to her room. I stood stock-still; he was the last person I wanted to encounter at that moment. I was about to turn back, but all at once curiosity held me rooted to the spot.

He had stopped in front of a mirror, smoothed his hair, and to my great surprise started humming a song. A dim childhood memory flashed into my mind. To make more understandable the curious sensation I experienced at that moment, I shall recount it here.

During my first year in that house, I had been profoundly impressed by a certain incident that became clear to me only at that moment when I saw Pyotr Aleksandrovich standing in front of the mirror; only then did I understand the origin of my inexplicable antipathy to the man. I have already mentioned that as a child I had always felt constrained in his presence, and have described the dismal impression made on me by his dour, preoccupied air, the expression of his face, which more often than not was melancholy and dejected, my distress after those hours spent at Aleksandra Mikhailovna's tea table, and how heartsick I had been when I had almost been forced to witness those ominous scenes that sometimes took place between them.

On that former occasion, I had come upon him in the identical way: in the same room, at the same hour, and as we were both on our way to see Aleksandra Mikhailovna. At that time I had felt a purely childish timidity on finding myself alone with him, and had guiltily hidden in a corner, praying that he would not notice me. Then, too, he had stopped in front of the mirror; but this second time, I shuddered with a vague but in no way childish feeling. Watching him on that earlier occasion, it had seemed to me that he was rearranging his face, for I had seen him smile as he approached the mirror and for the first time heard him laugh, and this had impressed me above all as he never laughed in his wife's presence. No sooner had he looked into the mirror than his face completely changed. The smile disappeared as at a word of command, and was replaced by an expression of bitterness. It was almost as if some emotion that was beyond human power to conceal had escaped from his

177

heart and, like a spasm of pain, distorted his lips, creased his brow, and contracted his eyebrows, despite his benevolent intention. He hid his morose look behind spectacles, and instantaneously became a different person. I recall that as a child I had trembled in fear and dread of understanding what I had seen, and from that time a disagreeable and distressing feeling had been irrevocably locked in my heart. After looking into the mirror for a moment, he had lowered his head and hunched his shoulders, which was his customary posture in his wife's presence, and proceeded on tiptoe to her sitting room. And that is the memory that had suddenly occurred to me.

On both occasions he had thought he was alone when he paused in front of the mirror. And on both occasions I had an unpleasant, antagonistic feeling on finding myself in his presence. But when I heard that humming—and from him, the last person from whom one would have expected such a thing—I was so taken by surprise that I was riveted to the spot; and when that moment reminded me of an almost identical moment in my childhood . . . I cannot describe what a violent effect this had on me. All my nerves began to quiver, and I reacted to that unfortunate humming by breaking into such a peal of laughter that the poor man cried out, recoiled a step or two from the mirror, and turned deathly pale, as though he had been ingnominiously caught committing a crime. He looked at me in a paroxysm of horror, astonishment, and rage. But his look had a disastrous effect on me, and, unable to control myself, I nervously, hysterically laughed in his face as I walked past him on my way to Aleksandra Mikhailovna's room.

I knew that he would probably stand behind the portieres, in doubt whether or not to follow me into the room—his wrath and cowardice would root him to the spot—and I waited with a certain exasperation and defiance to see what he would do. I was ready to wager that he would not come in, and I was right. He did not appear until half an hour later.

Aleksandra Mikhailovna gazed at me for some time in utter amazement, wondering what was the matter with me, but she questioned me in vain. I could not answer her, I was still struggling for breath. At last she realized that I was undergoing an attack of nerves and became concerned. When I was more composed, I took her hands and kissed them. Only then did I bethink myself; only then did it occur to me that I might have killed her had I not happened to encounter her husband just at that moment. I gazed at her as at someone risen from the dead.

When Pyotr Aleksandrovich came in, I gave him a fleeting glance; he looked as if nothing had happened between us, stern and sullen as usual. But from his pale face and the slight twitching at the corners of his mouth, I guessed that he was having difficulty concealing his agitation. He greeted Aleksandra Mikhailovna coldy and sat down in silence. His hands trembled when he took his cup of tea. I expected an outburst and was seized with fear. I would have gone to my room, but could not bring myself to leave Aleksandra Mikhailovna, whose face had changed the moment she looked at her husband. She sensed that something was wrong. At last what I had feared happened.

In the profound silence I raised my eyes and saw Pyotr Aleksandrovich peering at me through his spectacles. It was so unexpected that I started, almost screamed, and instantly lowered my eyes. Aleksandra Mikhailovna noticed my involuntary reaction.

"What's the matter with you? Why are you blushing?" Pyotr Aleksandrovich's shrill, harsh voice rang out.

I did not answer; my heart was beating so that I could not utter a word.

"Why is she blushing?" Why is she blushing?" he repeated, turning to Aleksandra Mikhailovna as he pointed to me contemptuously.

I gasped with indignation and looked at Aleksandra

Mikhailovna beseechingly. She understood me, and her pale cheeks instantly flamed.

"Anneta, go to your room," she said to me in a firm tone that was quite unexpected from her. "I'll come in a moment. We'll spend the evening together and——"

"I asked you a question—did you hear me or not?" Pyotr Aleksandrovich broke in, raising his voice still higher and apparently not listening to his wife. "Why do you blush when you encounter me? Answer!"

"Because you make her blush, as you do me," said Aleksandra Mikhailovna, her voice breaking with agitation.

I looked at her in amazement. The unwonted passion of her rejoinder was completely baffling to me.

"I make you blush—*I*?" Pyotr Alexandrovich's astonishment was so great that he was beside himself and vehemently stressed the word *I*. "*You* blush on account of *me*? It is for *you* to blush, but not on my account, don't you think?"

The significance of his words, spoken with such cruel and caustic mockery, was so clear to me that I cried out in horror and rushed to Aleksandra Mikhailovna's side. Pain, reproach, and horror were reflected in her face, which had turned deathly pale. I looked at Pyotr Aleksandrovich, my hands clasped imploringly. He himself seemed to realize what he had done, though the wrath that had wrung those words from him had not yet subsided. Seeing my silent entreaty, however, he was disconcerted. My gesture had betrayed my knowledge of what till then had been a secret between them, and showed quite clearly that I understood the meaning of what he had said to her.

"Anneta, go to your room," Aleksandra Mikhailovna repeated in a weak but steady voice, and she stood up. "Pyotr Aleksandrovich and I must have a talk."

She seemed calm, but I was more fearful of that calm than of any sort of agitation. I stood absolutely still, as if I had not heard her, and strained every nerve to read in her face what was going on in her heart at that moment. I felt that she had understood neither my exclamation nor my gesture.

"You see what you have done!" declared Pyotr Aleksandrovich, taking me by the arm as he pointed to his wife.

My God! Never have I seen such despair as was expressed in that stricken, ghastly face. I glanced back once more as he led me from the room. Aleksandra Mikhailovna was standing at the fireplace with her elbows on the mantel and both hands pressed tightly to her head. The posture of her whole body expressed the most unbearable torment. I grasped Pyotr Aleksandrovich's hand frantically.

"For God's sake!" I cried brokenly. "Have mercy!"

"Don't worry, don't worry!" he said, looking at me strangely. "It's nothing, she's just overwrought. Go along now, go along!"

When I reached my room I threw myself down on the sofa and buried my face in my hands. I lay there for three hours, and in that time lived through a complete inferno. At last I could bear it no longer and sent to ask whether I might go to Aleksandra Mikhailovna. Madame Leotard brought me the answer. Pyotr Aleksandrovich said that the attack had passed and there was nothing to worry about, but that Aleksandra Mikhailovna needed quiet. I did not go to bed before three o'clock in the morning, and all that time kept pacing the floor and thinking. My position was more perplexing than ever, but I felt somewhat calmer, perhaps because I felt that I was more guilty than anyone. At last I went to bed and waited impatiently for morning.

The next day, to my surprise and sorrow, I noticed an inexplicable coldness on the part of Aleksandra Mikhailovna. At first I thought that this pure and noble soul found it hard to be with me after my having witnessed the scene that had taken place the day before. I knew that this child was capable of blushing and asking *my* forgiveness for that unfortunate episode, which she perhaps felt had offended my sensibilities. But soon I noticed a very different sort of anxiety and vexation, which expressed itself most awkwardly. At times she answered me in a cold, dry tone; at other times there seemed to be some special meaning in what she said. And though she eventually became very affectionate with me, as if repenting of the severity that was so alien to her nature, nevertheless I sensed a reproach in her gentle, tender words.

Finally I asked her outright what was the matter and whether there was something she wished to say to me. She was taken aback by my abrupt question, and raising her large, gentle eyes to mine looked at me with a tender smile and said:

"No, nothing, Netochka. But, you know, when you asked me so suddenly, I was a little confused. It was only because your question was so abrupt, I assure you. But listen, tell me the truth, my child: is there anything in your heart that would cause you to be confused if someone were to question you in that unexpected way?"

"No," I replied, gazing into her clear eyes.

"Well, that's good! If you knew, my dear, how grateful I am to you for that splendid answer. Not that I would ever suspect you of any wrong—never! I could never forgive myself for even thinking such a thing. But, you know, I took you as a child, and now you are seventeen years old. You have seen for yourself that I am ill, that I am like a child and have to be looked after. I have not been able to be a real mother to you, though the abundance of love I have for you would have more than sufficed. If now I am tormented by worry, that, of course, is not your fault but my own. Forgive me both for the question and for having perhaps failed, in spite of myself, to keep all the promises I made to you and to Father when I took you to live here with me. This troubles me very much, my dear, and has often troubled me in the past."

I embraced her and burst into tears. "Oh, thank you, thank you for everything!" I said, my tears falling on her hands. "Don't say such things to me, don't break my heart. You were more than a mother to me. May God bless you and the Prince for all you have done for me, an abandoned pauper. My darling, my poor darling!"

"Enough, Netochka, enough! Come, put your arms around me; so, tighter, tighter! Do you know . . . God knows why, but I feel that you are embracing me for the last time."

"No, no!" I exclaimed, sobbing like a child. "No, that cannot be! You are going to be happy. . . . There are many days ahead. . . . Believe me, we'll be happy!"

"Thank you, thank you for your love. There are so few people around me now; everyone has deserted me!"

"Who has deserted you? Who?"

"There used to be others, Netochka, you don't know. They have all abandoned me, disappeared like phantoms. And I counted on them, all my life I counted on them. Well, never mind. . . . Look, Netochka: see how far we are into autumn. Soon there will be snow, and with the first snowfall I shall die . . . yes. But it doesn't grieve me. . . . Farewell!

Her face was pale and drawn; ominous crimson patches burned in her cheeks, and her quivering lips were parched from the fire within her.

She went to the piano, and as she struck a few chords, a string snapped and there was a prolonged, discordant twang.

"Do you hear, Netochka, do you hear?" she said, as if suddenly inspired. "That string was overstrained; it could not bear it and died. Do you hear how plaintively the sound dies?"

She spoke with difficulty, and her face reflected her suppressed mental anguish. There were tears in her eyes.

"Well, enough of that, Netochka, my dear, enough. Go and get the children."

I brought the children to her. She seemed to relax watching them, and after an hour let them go.

"You won't leave them when I die, will you Netochka?" she asked in a whisper, as though fearing someone might hear us.

"Stop, I can't bear it!" was all I could say in reply.

"But I was only jesting," she said after a momentary silence, and smiled. "You didn't believe me? Sometimes I talk such nonsense. I'm like a child now; everything must be forgiven me."

Then she glanced at me timidly, as though fearing to go on. I waited.

"Take care you don't upset him," she said at last, lowering her eyes and coloring slightly.

She spoke so softly I could hardly hear her.

"Who?" I asked in surprise.

"My husband. Please, tell him everything very gently."

"But why—why?" I repeated, in still greater surprise.

"Well, perhaps you won't even have to tell him . . . as it now seems," she said, slyly trying to observe me, though the same artless smile was on her lips and the color deepened in her face. "Enough of that. You know I am always jesting."

My heart again contracted painfully.

"Only listen, you will love them when I die, won't you?" she asked seriously, and added with a somewhat mysterious air: "As if they were your own children? Remember, I have always considered you as my own and have made no distinctions between you."

"Yes, yes," I responded, not knowing what I was saying and choked with tears and confusion.

I felt a burning kiss on my hand before I could withdraw it. Consternation left me tongue-tied.

"What is the matter with her? What is she thinking?" I wondered. "What happened yesterday between them?"

A moment later she complained of feeling tired.

"I've been ill for a long time, but I didn't want to alarm you both," she said. "After all, you both love me, don't you?. . . Good-bye, Netochka. Leave me now, but be sure to come back in the evening. You will, won't you?"

I promised to return, but was glad to leave: I could bear no more.

"Poor, poor thing!" I said to myself, sobbing. "Under what suspicion will you go to your grave? What new sorrow will wound and prey upon your heart without your daring to speak of it?" My God! That endless suffering, which by then I knew so well, that life without a ray of hope, that timid, undemanding love! And even now, when she was virtually on her deathbed, when her heart was riven with pain, she was as fearful of uttering the least murmur or complaint as if she were a criminal, and having imagined or invented some new sorrow was already accepting it and resigning herself to it.

That evening at twilight I took advantage of the absence of Ovrov (the visitor from Moscow) and went to the library. I opened one of the bookcases and began taking out the books, looking for something light and gay to read aloud to Aleksandra Mikhailovna in the hope of distracting her from her black thoughts. For a long time I glanced through the books absently. Dusk closed in, and with the darkness my despondency increased. Once more I found myself holding that same book in my hands, opened to the same page, where I again saw the outline of the letter whose secret I had borne within me and which seemed to have disrupted my life and begun it anew. It had enveloped me in so much that was cold, unknown, mysterious, and hostile, that I had begun to feel severely threatened.

"What will become of us?" I thought. "The nook in which I felt so cozy and at home will be empty! The pure, shining spirit who has watched over my youth will leave me. What lies ahead?"

I stood lost in thoughts of my past, now so dear to my heart, and at the same time strove to see ahead, into that unknown that was threatening me. . . . I recall that moment as if I were reliving it now, so deeply is it engraved in my memory.

I held both the letter and the open book in my hands, and my face was wet with tears. Suddenly I began to tremble with fear: I heard a familiar voice and at the same instant felt the letter being torn from my hands. I screamed, and looking up saw Pyotr Aleksandrovich standing before me. He seized me by the hand and would not let me go. With his right hand he held the letter up to the light, trying to make out the first lines. I cried out; I would rather have died than to have left that letter in his hands. I saw by his triumphant smile that he had succeeded in making out the first line. I lost my head. . . .

Almost beside myself, I snatched the letter from his hand. It all happened so quickly that I did not understand how I had retrieved the letter. But seeing that he was about to take it from me again, I thrust it into the bodice of my dress and recoiled two or three paces.

For a moment we looked at each other in silence. I was still trembling with fear. He was pale, his lips blue and quivering with rage. At last he broke the silence.

"Enough!" he said in a voice weak with emotion. "I suppose you don't want me to use force, so give me the letter of your own accord."

Only then did I stop to think, and I was outraged, filled with shame and indignation at the idea of brute force. The hot tears streamed down my burning cheeks. I was trembling all over and momentarily incapable of uttering a word.

"Did you hear me?" he said, taking a step or two toward me.

"Leave me alone, leave me alone!" I cried, recoiling. "You are behaving contemptibly, dishonorably. You forget your-self!. . . Let me pass!"

"What? What does this mean? You still dare to take such a tone with me—after you—— Give it to me. I tell you!"

He again advanced toward me, but looking into my eyes saw such determination that he hesitated.

"Very well!" he said dryly, as though having arrived at a decision, yet hardly able to restrain himself. "That will come in due course, but first . . ."

He looked around the room.

"You—— Who let you into the library? Why is that bookcase open? Where did you get the key?"

"I will not answer you," I said. "I cannot talk to you. Let me go now."

I went to the door.

"If you please!" he said, taking hold of my arm and stopping me. "You are not going like that."

I wrenched my arm free of his grasp and again moved toward the door.

"Very well, then. But I cannot allow you to receive letters from your lovers in my house."

I cried out, aghast, and looked at him in utter bewilderment.

"And therefore——"

"Stop!" I cried. "How can you—how can you say that to me?. . . My God, my God!"

"What? Are you still threatening me?"

I gazed at him, stricken with despair.

The scene between us had attained a degree of cruelty that I was at a loss to comprehend. My look implored him to go no further. I was ready to forgive his insult if he would cease. He gazed at me fixedly and in apparent uncertainty.

"Don't push me too far!" I whispered in horror.

"No, this must end!" he said at last, as if having reconsidered. "I confess, your look gave me pause for a moment," he added with a strange smile. "But, unfortunately, the matter speaks for itself. I managed to read the beginning of the letter. It is a love letter. You will not persuade me otherwise—no, you can put that out of your mind! And if I was momentarily in doubt, it only proves that to all your other excellent qualities I must add a talent for lying, and therefore, I repeat. . . "

As he talked, his face became more and more distorted with malice. He turned pale; his lips twitched and quivered, till at last he was hardly able to articulate. It was growing dark. I stood there, defenseless and alone, with a man who was capable of insulting a woman. And appearances were all against me, after all. I suffered agonies of shame; I was bewildered, and could not understand the spitefulness of the man. Without answering him, I fled from the room, distraught with horror.

Before I knew it, I found myself standing outside the door to Aleksandra Mikhailovna's sitting room. I heard her footsteps and was about to enter the room when I stopped as if thunderstruck.

"What will this do to her?" flashed into my mind. "That letter!. . . No, anything .. the world rather than this final blow to her heart!"

And I quickly turned to go, but it was too late; he stood there beside me.

"Come, let us go—wherever you wish—only not here, not here!" I whispered, seizing his hand. "Have mercy on her! I'll go back to the library, or wherever you say! You will kill her!"

"It is you who will kill her!" he replied, thrusting me aside.

All my hopes vanished. I felt that to place the whole thing before Aleksandra Mikhailovna was the very thing he wanted.

"For God's sake!" I said, trying with all my might to hold him back.

But at that moment the portières were parted and Aleksandra Mikhailovna appeared. She looked at us in surprise. Her face was more pallid than ever, and she could hardly stand on her feet. It had obviously cost her a great effort to come to the door when she heard our voices.

"Who is there? What are you talking about?" she asked, looking at us in utter amazement.

There was a prolonged silence, and she turned pale as a sheet. I rushed to her, threw my arms around her and drew her back into the sitting room. Pyotr Aleksandrovich followed. I hid my face in her bosom and clung to her, numb with dread.

"What is it? What's the matter with you both?" asked Aleksandra Mikhailovna a second time.

"Ask her. Only yesterday you came to her defense," said Pyotr Aleksandrovich, dropping heavily into a chair.

I continued to hold her in my firm embrace.

"My God, what is this?" exclaimed Aleksandra Mikhailovna in terrible dismay. "You are so upset, and she is frightened to death. Anneta, tell me what has happened between you."

"No, permit me to speak first," said Pyotr Aleksandrovich, and coming to us took me by the arm and pulled me away from Aleksandra Mikhailovna. "Stand there," he said, pointing to the middle of the room. "I intend to judge you in the presence of the woman who has been a mother to you. And you will please calm yourself and sit down," he added, seating Aleksandra Mikhailovna in an armchair. "It grieves me that I cannot spare you this distressing explanation, but it is unavoidable."

"My God! What can it be?" Aleksandra Mikhailovna ex-

exclaimed in acute despair, looking in turn from her husband to me.

I was wringing my hands in anticipation of the fateful moment. I could expect no mercy from him.

"In a word," continued Pyotr Aleksandrovich, "I should like to have you join me in passing judgment on her. You always—and I don't know why, it's one of your fantasies—you always—even yesterday, for instance—have thought and said—— But, I don't know how to say it, I blush at the supposition—— In a word, you have been defending her, and attacking me. You have accused me of *undue* severity. You have further hinted at a rather *different feeling*, as if provoking me to this undue severity. You—but I do not understand why I cannot suppress my embarrassment, this reddening at the thought of your suggestion, why I cannot speak of it frankly and openly before her. In a word, you——"

"Oh, you wouldn't—no, you will not say that!" cried Aleksandra Mikhailovna in terrible agitation and burning with shame. "No, spare her. It was I—I invented the whole thing! I have absolutely no suspicions now. Forgive me for them, forgive me! I am ill, I must be forgiven, only don't say that to her, no!... Anneta," she said, rising and coming to me, "Anneta, go away from here, quickly, quickly! He was only joking, it is I who am guilty of everything. This is a most inappropriate jest."

"In a word, you were jealous of me because of her," said Pyotr Aleksandrovich, mercilessly flinging out the words in response to her anguished expectation.

She screamed, blanched, and, hardly able to stand, clung to a chair for support.

"God forgive you!" she finally murmured in a faint voice. "Forgive me, Netochka, forgive me. It was all my fault. I was ill, I——"

"But this is brutal—it's shameless, vile!" I cried frantically, understanding at last why he had wanted to denounce me before his wife. "It's beneath contempt, you——"

"Anneta!" cried Aleksandra Mikhailovna, seizing my hand.

"A farce, nothing but a farce!" declared Pyotr Aleksandrovich, coming up to us in indescribable excitement. "A farce, I tell you," he went on, looking at his wife with a vindictive smile, "and the only person who has been deceived by all this is—you! I assure you that *we,*" he continued breathlessly, as he pointed to me, " *we* are not so afraid of such scenes. I assure you that *we* are not so chaste as to be offended, to blush and cover our ears when someone starts talking to us of such matters. You must excuse me, I express myself simply, directly, crudely perhaps, but that's how it must be. Are you convinced, madam, of the proper behavior of this . . . maiden?"

"My God! What is the matter with you? You forget yourself!" exclaimed Aleksandra Mikhailovna, staggered and livid with fear.

"Please," Pyotr Aleksandrovich broke in, "omit the highflown language. I don't care for it. What we are dealing with is something plain, simple, and vulgar in the extreme. I am asking you about her conduct. Do you know——"

But I did not let him finish, and grasping his arm drew him aside. In another moment all might have been lost.

"Do not speak of the letter!" I said in a whisper. "You will kill her on the spot. To reproach me is to reproach her. She cannot be my judge, because . . . I know everything . . . you understand, *everything!*"

He gazed at me with intense, undisguised curiosity. Suddenly he became confused and the blood rushed to his face.

"I know *everything, everything!*" I repeated.

He looked uncertain. His lips formed a question, but I forestalled it.

"What happened was this," I said aloud, hastily turning to

Aleksandra Mikhailovna, who was gazing at us with timid, wistful bewilderment. "I am completely guilty. It was four years ago when I first began deceiving you. I got hold of the key to the library, and for four years now I have been reading the books in secret. Pyotr Aleksandrovich caught me with one which . . .which should never have fallen into my hands. In his alarm for me, he exaggerated the danger to you. But I am not justifying myself," I hastened to add, seeing the mocking smile on his lips. "I am completely guilty. The temptation was too great for me, and, having sinned, I was ashamed to confess my wrongdoing. . . . That is all, almost all that happened between us."

"Oh, how clever!" whispered Pyotr Aleksandrovich, who was standing near me.

Aleksandra Mikhailovna listened to me with profound attention, but her disbelief was clearly apparent in her face. She looked now at her husband, now at me. No one spoke. I could hardly breathe. She lowered her head and covered her eyes with her hand, evidently weighing every word I had said. At last she raised her head and gazed at me intently.

"Netochka, my child, I know you are incapable of lying," she said. "Is that all that happened, absolutely all?"

"All," I answered.

"Is it all?" she asked, turning to her husband.

"Yes, that's all," he replied with an effort.

I felt relieved.

"Will you give me your word, Netochka?"

"Yes," I answered without faltering.

I could not help glancing at Pyotr Aleksandrovich. He had laughed when I gave my word. I flushed and my embarrassment was obvious to poor Aleksandra Mikhailovna. Her crushing, tormenting misery was reflected in her face.

"Enough," she said sadly. "I believe you. I cannot do otherwise."

"I think such a confession suffices," announced Pyotr Aleksandrovich. "You have heard her. And what, may I ask, do you think?"

Aleksandra Mikhailovna did not reply. The situation was becoming increasingly difficult.

"Tomorrow I shall look over all the books," Pyotr Aleksandrovich resumed. "I don't know what was there, but ——"

"What was the book she was reading?" asked Aleksandra Mikhailovna.

"The book? You tell her," he said to me. "You will know better how to *explain the matter,*" he added with a barely concealed sneer.

I was flustered and could not utter a word. Aleksandra Mikhailovna blushed and lowered her eyes. There was a long pause. Pyotr Aleksandrovich paced the room in exasperation.

"I do not know what took place between you," Aleksandra Mikhailovna at last began, hesitantly bringing out each word, "but if it was *only that,*" she went on, endeavoring to give special meaning to every word, and, though trying not to look at him, disconcerted by her husband's fixed stare, "if it was *only that,* then I do not know what cause we have for such grief or despair. I am more guilty than anyone—I alone, and this is a severe trial to me. I have neglected her upbringing, and I ought to answer for everything. She must forgive me, and I cannot, dare not, judge her. But, I repeat, what cause have we to despair? The danger has passed. Look at her," she said, growing more and more animated and turning to her husband with a searching glance, "look at her: can her imprudent act have had any consequence whatever? Can it be that I do not know her, my child, my dear daughter? That I do not know her pure and noble heart, and that in this pretty little head," she continued, drawing me to her and caressing me, "there is a bright, clear mind, a conscience that shrinks from deception?... Enough, my dears! Let us drop this now! Truly, there must be something else behind our distress; perhaps the shadow of animosity rested upon us momentarily. But we shall dispel it with love, and with kindness and harmony dispel our perplexity. Perhaps there is much we have withheld, and for this I blame myself. I was the first to conceal something when Heaven knows what suspicions sprang up in me, for which my sick mind is to blame. But . . . but, if now we have spoken out even partly, then you must both forgive me, because . . . because, after all, there is no great sin in my having been suspicious."

When she had finished, she blushed and glanced timorously at her husband, awaiting his response.

A mocking smile had appeared on his face as he listened to her. He left off pacing the room and stood directly in front of her, his hands clasped behind his back, apparently contemplating her confusion with admiration. She was further disconcerted by his intent gaze. He waited a moment as if expecting her to go on. Her confusion was redoubled. At last he broke the oppressive silence with a long, low, taunting laugh.

"You poor woman, I feel very sorry for you," he said at last, seriously, bitterly, and no longer laughing. "You have taken upon yourself a role that is beyond you. What did you want? Did you want to provoke me to an answer, to incite me with new suspicions, or rather, the old suspicions, which your words failed to conceal? The sense of what you have said is that there is no reason to be angry with her, that she is good even after reading immoral books—the morality of which, speaking for myself, seems to have had a certain success already—that, in fact, you yourself are responsible for her. Is that what you mean? Well then, explain this: you hinted at something else; you seem to think that my suspicion and persecution arise from another sort of feeling. You even implied yesterday—please don't stop me, I like speaking plainly— you even implied yesterday that in certain people—I recall that in your observation these people more often than not are sedate, austere, upright, intelligent, strong, and God knows what other attributes you ascribed to them in your access of magnanimity —that in certain people, I repeat, love—and God only knows where you got this idea—can only be expressed vehemently, harshly, grimly, often with suspicion and persecution. I really do not remember very well whether this is exactly what you said yesterday. . . .Please, don't stop me; I know your protégée very well: she can hear it all, all, I repeat it a hundred times—all. You are deceived. But I do not know why you like to insist that I am exactly that sort of person. God knows why you want to deck me out in fools' motley. I am hardly of an age to love that girl, and, for that matter, you may be assured, madam, that *I know my duty,* and however magnanimously you may have apologized to me, I will say as before: *regardless of the degree of sublimity to which you may have elevated a depraved feeling, a crime will always be a crime, a sin remains a sin, shameful, vile, ignoble.* But enough! Enough! And I'll hear no more about these abominations."

Aleksandra Mikhailovna wept.

"Well, let me bear this, let the sin be mine!" she said at last, sobbing and embracing me. "Would it were my suspicions that were shameful; would that you had derided them so harshly. . . . But you poor child, why have you been condemned to hear such insults? And I am unable to defend you! I am mute! My God!. . . I cannot remain silent, sir! I will not tolerate—— Your conduct is insane!"

"Don't, don't!" I whispered, trying to calm her agitation, fearing that her severe recriminations might further incense him. I was quaking with fear for her.

"You blind woman!" he shouted. "You do not know, you do not see——"

He paused momentarily.

"Get away from her!" he said, turning to me and tearing my hand out of hers. "I will not allow you to touch my wife; you defile her; your presence is an insult to her! But what is it that compels me to be silent, when I should speak, when it is imperative that I speak?" he cried, stamping his foot. "And I will speak, I will tell everything. I do not know what you *know,* madam, and what you were trying to threaten me with, nor do I wish to know. But, listen!" he said to his wife. "Just listen!"

"Be still!" I cried, rushing forward. "Be still! Not a word!"

"Listen——"

"Silence, in the name of ——"

"In the name of what?" he broke in, and with a swift, penetrating look into my eyes repeated: "In the name of what?... I want you to know that I took from her hands a letter from a lover! That is what has been going on under our roof! That is what has been happening under your very nose—which you did not see, of which you were oblivious!"

I was scarcely able to stand. Aleksandra Mikhailovna turned pale as a ghost.

"That cannot be," she said in a scarcely audible whisper.

"I saw the letter, madam; it was in my hands; I read the first lines, and it was unmistakably a letter from a lover. She snatched it from my hands. She has it now—it is clear what it is, beyond any doubt. And if you still doubt it, look at her, and then try to hope for even the shadow of a doubt."

"Netochka!" cried Aleksandra Mikhailovna, rushing toward me. "But no, do not speak, do not speak! I do not know what—how it—my God, my God!"

And she buried her face in her hands and began to sob.

"But no! It cannot be!" she cried again. "You are mistaken. This ... I know what this means!" she exclaimed, looking intently at her husband. "You—I—could not—you are not deceiving me, you cannot deceive me! Tell me, tell me everything frankly. He was mistaken—he was, wasn't he? He saw something else, he was blinded. He was, wasn't he? Wasn't he?. . . Come, why won't you tell me everything, Anneta, my child, my own darling child?"

"Answer, answer at once!" Pyotr Aleksandrovich's voice rang out. "Tell her: did I or did I not see the letter in your hands?"

"Yes!" I said, breathless with agitation.

"Was it a letter from your lover?"

"Yes!" I replied.

"With whom you are still in contact?"

"Yes, yes, yes!" I said, beside myself and answering yes to everything to end our torture.

"You have heard her. Well, what do you say now? Believe me, you kind, too trusting soul," he added, taking his wife's hand, "believe me, and do not be deluded by all that was born in your sick imagination. Now you see what this . . . *maiden* is. I only wanted to prove to you how incongruous your suspicions were. I observed all this long ago, and am glad for your sake that I have at last brought it into the open. It was painful for me to see her with you, in your embrace, sitting at the same table with us, and, for that matter, living in my house. I was outraged by your blindness. That is the reason, and that is the only reason, I took any notice of her, kept my eye on her, and it was this attention that struck you, and, with some bizarre suspicion as a starting point you then embroidered God knows what on this canvas. But now the situation has come to a head and there is no longer any doubt. And tomorrow," he concluded, turning to me, "tomorrow you will leave my house!"

"Stop!" cried Aleksandra Mikhailovna, half rising from her chair. "I do not believe all this. Don't look at me so fiercely, and don't mock me. Now I will ask you to hear my opinion. Anneta, my child, come here, give me your hand, so. We are all sinners!" she said in a tearful voice, humbly glancing at her husband. "And who of us can refuse another's hand? So give me your hand, Anneta, my dear child. I am no better, no more worthy than you; you cannot insult me with your presence, because I too, *I too am a sinner.*"

"Madam!" cried Pyotr Aleksandrovich in amazement. "Madam! Restrain yourself! Do not forget——"

"I forget nothing. Don't interrupt me, and let me finish. You saw a letter in her hands; you even read it. You say, and she admits, that it was a letter from someone she loves. But does this really prove that she has done wrong? Does it give you the right to treat her like this, to degrade her in the eyes of your wife? Yes, sir, in the eyes of your wife. Had you perhaps considered the matter? And do you really know how it was?"

"So it remains for me to run and ask her forgiveness—is that what you want?" shouted Pyotr Aleksandrovich. "I no longer have the patience to listen to you! Think what you're saying. Do you know what you are talking about? Do you know what and *whom* you are defending? But I see through it all——"

"You don't see the first thing, because your pride and anger prevent you from seeing. You see neither what I am defending nor what I am trying to say. I am not defending evil. But had you considered that, being a child, she is perhaps innocent? No, I am not defending evil! I hasten to make this reservation, if that will satisfy you. Yes, if she were a wife and mother and had forgotten her duty—oh, then I would have agreed with you. . . . You see, I have made a reservation. Take note of it and don't reproach me. But if she received this letter not knowing it was wrong? If she was carried away because of her inexperience and there was no one to restrain her? If I am the most guilty because I failed to watch over her? If this was the first letter? If you have insulted her pure, virginal feelings with your coarse suspicions? If you have sullied her imagination with your cynical talk about this letter? If you did not see that chaste, maidenly shame glowing in her face, pure as the innocence which I see now, and which I saw when she was mortified and tortured, not knowing what to say, and, racked with anguish, answered by admitting to all your cruel, inhuman accusations? Yes, yes! It is inhuman and cruel. I do not recognize you. I shall never forgive you for this—never!"

"Have mercy on me, have mercy on me!" I cried, clinging to her. "Have mercy, believe me, don't reject me——"

I fell to my knees at her feet.

"If, in fact," she continued in a choked voice, "I had not been at her side, and if you had frightened her with your words and made the poor child believe she was guilty; if you had confused her conscience, her soul, and destroyed her peace of mind—my God! You would have turned her out of the house! Do you know whom you would have had to deal with? Do you know that if you turn her out of the house you turn us both out—me as well? . . . Did you hear me, sir?"

Her eyes flashed; her bosom heaved; the agonizing strain led to the final crisis.

"I have heard quite enough, madam!" cried Pyotr Aleksandrovich at last. "Enough of this! I know, of course, that there is such a passion known as Platonic love, know it to my sorrow, madam—do you hear? To my sorrow! But I am unable to live with gilded sin. I do not understand it. Away with trumpery! And if you feel that you are guilty, if you know something about yourself—it is not for me to remind you of it, madam. In short, if the thought of leaving my house is so appealing to you, then I can only say that it is too bad you neglected to carry out your intention at the proper time, at that time a year ago—if you have forgotten, let me remind you——"

I glanced at Aleksandra Mikhailovna. She suddenly leaned on me, convulsed with grief, her eyes half-closed with untold agony. A moment later she collapsed.

"Oh, for God's sake, spare her now at least! Do not speak the final word," I cried, falling on my knees at Pyotr Aleksandrovich's feet, not realizing that I was betraying myself.

But it was too late. In response to my words, a faint cry was heard, and the poor woman fell to the floor unconscious.

"It's all over! You have killed her!" I said. "Call the maids, save her! I shall go to the study and wait for you there. I must talk to you. I will tell you everything."

"But what? What?"

"Later."

The fainting fit lasted for two hours. The entire household was in a state of consternation. The doctor shook his head doubtfully.

At the end of those two hours, I went to Pyotr Aleksandrovich's study. He had just come from his wife and was pacing the room and biting his fingernails down to the quick. He looked pale and distracted; I had never seen him like that before.

"What did you want to tell me?" he asked in a stern, brusque voice. "You wanted to say something?"

"That letter which you snatched from my hands—will you recognize it?"

"Yes."

"Here, take it."

He took the letter and held it up to the light. I watched him intently. A few minutes later he quickly turned to the fourth page and looked at the signature. I could see the blood rush to his head.

"Well, what is it?" he asked, looking dumbfounded.

"Three years ago, when I found this letter in a book, I guessed that it had been forgotten; I read it and ... knew everything. And from that day I kept it because there was no one I could give it to. I could not have given it to her. And you? But you must have known the contents of the letter, in which there was the whole sad story. . . . I do not know what the purpose of your pretense may be. That is a mystery to me. I am still unable to understand your dark soul. You have wanted to maintain your superiority over her, and you have done so. But why? In order to triumph over a phantom, over the distracted imagination of a sick woman; in order to prove to her that she had strayed and you were *more virtuous* than she! And you accomplished your aim, for that suspicion of hers—the fixed idea that dimmed her mind— is perhaps the final lament of a broken heart over the injustice of that condemnation with which you were in accord. 'What was wrong with your falling in love with me?' is what she was saying, what she wanted to show you. Your vanity, your jealous egoism, were merciless. Good-bye! No explanations are necessary. But, take care, I know you through and through, and don't forget it!"

I went to my room, hardly knowing what had happened to me. I was stopped at the door by Ovrov, who had been assisting Pyotr Aleksandrovich with his business affairs.

"I should like to talk to you," he said, bowing politely.

I looked at him, scarcely understanding what he had said.

"Later. . . . You must excuse me, I am not feeling well," I replied, as I passed him.

"Tomorrow, then," he said, retiring with a rather ambiguous smile.

But perhaps I only imagined it. . . . All this seemed to have flashed before my eyes.

—1848